April 2019

Peterson Middle School
1380 Rosalia Ave
Sunnyvale, CA 94087
SCUSD

THE CAVE

"You guys—*listen!*" Jane said, louder than before. The urgency in her voice was unmistakable.

"What is it?" Buzz asked.

"There's something in here," Jane said.

Carter ducked his head to listen. The rain outside poured down, but the sounds in the cave seemed to bounce off one another and amplify. And that's when he heard it. A soft rustling of some kind was coming from deeper inside. Something was moving around back there. It sent a fresh wave of goose bumps down his arms.

"Everyone get up . . . slowly," he said. "Vanessa, you got the light?"

"Got it," she said. She'd turned off the flashlight to save the batteries, but she clicked it back on now. The beam shook unsteadily as she played it across the cave walls.

Then, before the light could show them anything, a piercing scream broke out of the darkness. For a split second, Carter thought it was Jane—but she was right there next to him. The sound was farther away than that. And in fact, he realized, it hadn't been a human voice at all. It was an animal.

He and Vanessa looked at each other.

"Run!" Vanessa shouted.

The STRANDED Series

STRANDED 2
TRIAL BY FIRE

JEFF PROBST
and CHRIS TEBBETTS

PUFFIN BOOKS
An Imprint of Penguin Group (USA)

PUFFIN BOOKS
An imprint of Penguin Young Readers Group
Published by the Penguin Group
Penguin Group (USA)
375 Hudson Street
New York, New York 10014, U.S.A.

USA / Canada / UK / Ireland / Australia / New Zealand / India / South Africa / China
Penguin Books Ltd, Registered Offices: 80 Strand, London WC2R 0RL, England

For more information about the Penguin Group visit www.penguin.com

First published in the United States of America by Puffin Books,
an imprint of Penguin Young Readers Group, 2013
This edition published by Puffin Books,
an imprint of Penguin Young Readers Group, 2013

LIBRARY OF CONGRESS CIP DATA IS AVAILABLE

Puffin Books ISBN 978-0-14-751195-9 (Hardcover)

Design by Tony Sahara
Set in Century Schoolbook

Printed in the United States of America

1 3 5 7 9 10 8 6 4 2

The publisher does not have any control over and does not assume
any responsibility for author or third-party websites or their content.

To those courageous enough to seek their adventure.

Be Bold. Dream Big.

For the adventure you're ready for . . .

is the one you get

—JP

CHAPTER 1

Vanessa forced herself to take another step. Then another. And another. It was everything she could do to keep from dropping to her knees in the mud and giving up. But that was the last thing any of them could afford.

It was the second huge storm in a week. The first had crashed their fifty-foot sailboat, the *Lucky Star,* onto the rocky shore of this tiny island. Now another one had come along and dragged the boat—their only shelter—back out to sea. The four of them had been lucky to get off alive as they'd scrambled over the rocks, onto the beach, and up into the jungle.

"Keep moving! And stay together!" she shouted to the others. Her voice was already hoarse, trying to be heard over the wind, and thunder, and crashing waves. She held her flashlight out in front of her, but it was hard to see. The rain poured down in sheets, even under the jungle's thick canopy of trees.

They moved in a tight clump, holding on to one another and to the few things they'd managed to take. Jane and Buzz stayed close on either side. Carter was right behind, pushing the group to go faster. Behind them, Vanessa could hear the tide pounding the shore, each wave a little higher than the one before it. If they didn't keep heading uphill, it was going to be one of them who got washed away next.

"I think I dropped something!" Jane called.

"Leave it!" Vanessa told her. "Don't stop!"

"But—"

"I said leave it!"

She didn't like yelling at Jane, even now, but it couldn't be helped. The only thing that mattered was finding shelter. And that meant getting to the caves as fast as possible.

The island was run through with them, like some kind of giant underground maze. The closest cavern opening they'd found was only a minute's walk up from the beach. But that was during the day, and in the light. Now the cave seemed impossibly far off as they shuffled along, tripping over roots and rocks and squinting through the heaviest downpour Vanessa had ever seen.

"Just keep moving!" she shouted. "It's going to be okay! It's going to be—"

The words caught in her throat with a sob. The truth was, Vanessa had no idea if it was going to be okay or not. How was a thirteen-year-old supposed to handle something like this? Still, Buzz and Carter were eleven, and Jane was only nine. Without any parents or other adults around, it was up to her to keep the three younger ones safe for as long as possible. That much Vanessa knew.

But knowing it and doing it were two very different things.

Carter gritted his teeth. It wasn't as if Vanessa, Buzz, or Jane could see him in the dark, but he knew he had to stay strong. This wasn't a place where you could let your guard down, even for a second.

As they trudged uphill, he kept one hand on his little sister's shoulder and another on the pillowcase he'd used as a makeshift pack. It was heavy with the fire axe from the *Lucky Star*, along with some sea charts and whatever else he'd scooped off the galley table in the dark. There hadn't been time to pick and choose. They'd taken whatever they could before the boat was swept away. Everything else was lost.

Meanwhile, the cold wind off the Pacific seemed to cut right through his soaking-wet clothes. He couldn't stop shivering—and neither could Jane. If there was any good news, it was that the ground had started to level off underfoot. That meant they were getting close.

Sure enough, with the next flash of lightning,

Carter saw just ahead a familiar rock wall and the arched black opening of the cave itself. It was huge, maybe two stories high and wide enough for a truck to turn around inside. It wouldn't be any warmer in there, but at least it would be dry.

"Straight ahead! Did you see that?" he shouted.

No one answered, but they all picked up their pace. The small beam of Vanessa's flashlight led the way across the last twenty yards of flat muddy ground.

As they passed under the rock overhang and into the cave's entrance, Carter felt the rain lighten to a sprinkle, then down to nothing at all. Finally, a break. Vanessa, Jane, and Buzz all sank to the ground, heaving for breath in the dark.

"Keep going!" Carter said. The wind was still bad at the front of the cave. There was no sense stopping now.

"Give us a second," Vanessa told him.

"Just a little farther," Carter said. "It's freezing right here!"

"Um . . . you guys?" Jane said.

"It's freezing everywhere. Calm down!" Vanessa said. Even now, she had to be the boss. It was like she couldn't help it.

"*You* calm down!" Carter snapped, just before Jane cut them both off.

"You guys—*listen!*" she said, louder than before. The urgency in her voice was unmistakable.

"What is it?" Buzz asked.

"There's something in here," Jane said.

Carter ducked his head to listen. The rain outside poured down, but the sounds in the cave seemed to bounce off one another and amplify. And that's when he heard it. A soft rustling of some kind was coming from deeper inside. Something was moving around back there. It sent a fresh wave of goose bumps down his arms.

"Everyone get up . . . slowly," he said. "Vanessa, you got the light?"

"Got it," she said. She'd turned off the flashlight to save the batteries, but she clicked it back on now. The beam shook unsteadily as she played it across the cave walls.

Then, before the light could show them anything, a piercing scream broke out of the darkness. For a split second, Carter thought it was Jane—but she was right there next to him. The sound was farther away than that. And in fact, he realized, it hadn't been a human voice at all. It was an animal.

He and Vanessa looked at each other.

"Run!" Vanessa shouted.

As she turned to go, she tripped and fell. The flashlight dropped out of her hand. In the next moment they were all thrown into inky pitch blackness—just as Carter spotted the shadow of something on four legs bolting straight at them from the back of the cave.

And behind it were several others, all screaming as they came.

Something big slammed into Jane as it ran past her in the dark. It sent a shock wave of pain through her arm. Her hand slipped out of Carter's, and she spun around as she fell, scraping her knees and palms over the rocky ground.

"Carter!" she yelled.

"Jane? Where are you?"

It was impossible to see through the darkness, much less to try to reach her brother. The stampede of beasts—whatever they were—pounded all around them now. Jane could feel their feet thudding on either side of her. She tried to crawl away toward the wall on one side just as one of them raced by. She then moved in the opposite direction, only to be knocked to the ground a second time. There was nowhere to go. All she could do was curl into a ball with her knees drawn up tight, and hope not to get completely trampled.

The worst part was the noise. Even with her hands over her ears, it filled Jane's head—a humanlike, squealing sound straight out of a horror movie. It seemed to go on and on, echoing off the cave walls and high ceiling. She let out a scream of her own, but it only mixed in with the others until she couldn't hear herself at all.

Then, as quickly as it had begun, the sounds faded. The thudding feet grew softer. The squealing came from outside now, and trailed off into the night.

Jane's heart was still pounding when she moved her hands away from her ears and tried to look around.

"Carter?" she said again. "Vanessa? Buzz?"

"I'm here," Carter answered. He was closer than she'd realized. Somehow that made her feel a little better. "Is everyone okay?"

"I'm okay," Buzz said, though his voice sounded shaky.

"Me, too," Vanessa answered. Jane could sense them all crawling toward her, feeling their way, but it was impossible to see.

"Where's the flashlight?" she asked.

A few soft clicking noises came from nearby. And then, "I think it's broken," Vanessa answered.

This wasn't like any darkness Jane had ever experienced at home. Not like when she turned off her bedside light to go to sleep at night. At least then, you could see your hand in front of your face. Here, the only comfort at all came from the sound of the others' voices. As soon as Carter found her, she wrapped her arms around him and held on tight. She squeezed her eyes shut in the dark, trying to cut off the tears, but they wouldn't stop. After everything that had just happened, it was hard not to wonder, *What else? What next?*

Vanessa and Buzz were close behind. They clustered in tightly now with Carter and Jane. All four of them were still shaking badly.

"What were those things, anyway?" Carter asked.

"Wild boars," Jane answered. "That's what they had to be."

She'd seen pictures of them back home, and even a video about boar hunting in the South Pacific. The boars were like wild pigs, big and strong with tusks and sharp teeth. It was lucky none of them had been hurt, or completely trampled. Jane shivered with the thought of what could have happened.

"They were probably trying to get out of the storm, too," she said. "I'll bet we took their spot."

"What if they want it back?" Buzz asked.

"Let's hope they don't," Carter answered. There wasn't much to say to that. All they could really do now was stick close together, wait for daylight, and hope for the best.

As Jane hunkered in with the others, teeth chattering in the dark, wet clothes sticking to her skin, it all started to sink in. These last three days on the island had been the worst of her life, by far. The worst of *any* of their lives. They'd barely had enough food, and they'd practically killed themselves finding water. So far, there had been no sign of rescue, and no way of knowing if help was coming anytime soon. Or at all. It had been just the four of them living alone on the wreck of the *Lucky Star*.

Now even the boat was gone, along with the last of their food and almost everything else they'd had on board. All of which could mean only one thing. Their lives here were about to get harder.

Much, much harder.

CHAPTER 2

The rain stopped sometime just before dawn.

Buzz was the first to notice. It was the sound that changed. The wind died down first, and then the steady drumbeat of the rain itself. Finally, the darkness lifted, and the shape of the cave's mouth started to show in the very earliest morning light.

Carter, Vanessa, and Jane were sitting with their heads drooped, half awake. None of them had slept, not really, but they didn't seem ready to get up and move yet, either.

Still, nature called. Buzz had been holding on for what felt like hours. After the run-in with the boars, who knew what else might be waiting out there?

But the rocks dug into his back no matter how he sat, and his damp clothes had kept him shivering through the night. It was crazy how cold it got here after dark, considering how hot it was during the day. He'd never been this cold in his life, not even during the worst Chicago winters back home.

Finally, he got up, stretched his aching body, and stepped outside.

The ground around the cave's entrance was littered with the things they'd brought from the boat. They'd dropped most of it in the confusion, including the two blankets Buzz had grabbed. Those were both filthy now, and trampled into the mud, with dozens of small hoofprints all around.

As he headed downhill to look for a private spot, Buzz found a few more of their things. There was a coil of rope that Carter had been carrying. A crumpled-up sea chart under a bush. A single shoe stuck in the mud.

And then, just before he reached the beach, he

spotted Jane's bright yellow waterproof camera. It sat under the palm tree where they'd stopped to regroup.

Jane was going to be thrilled. She'd brought the camera to the South Pacific to make a video report for her fifth-grade class, all about the trip they were meant to take.

That is, until everything went so wrong.

It was supposed to be a week of open-ocean sailing with their uncle Dexter and his first mate, Joe Kahali, while their parents honeymooned in Hawaii. Two months earlier, Buzz and Vanessa's father had married Carter and Jane's mother. The whole idea of the sailing adventure was to give their parents some alone time while the kids got to know one another better as brothers and sisters.

Now Dex and Joe were out there on a life raft somewhere, hopefully still alive. Their parents were a thousand miles away in Hawaii. And Vanessa, Buzz, Jane, and Carter had been forced to fend for themselves here on Nowhere Island. That was Jane's name for it—Nowhere Island—because as far as they knew, this place wasn't on anyone's map. The only communication they'd managed was a quick conversation with the Coast Guard in Hawaii, and even that had been cut short when their satellite phone had died. Whether or not the authorities would be able to find this uncharted island in the middle of nowhere, Buzz had no idea.

Coming out of the woods and onto the beach, he scanned the horizon. As usual, all he saw was an endless stretch of sea and sky. No boats, no planes, nothing.

From the beach, Buzz climbed up onto the black volcanic rocks they'd scrambled off of the night before. They called this spot Dead Man's Shelf. It was where the *Lucky Star* had crashed. Now the only signs that their boat had been there at all were the few stray pieces of junk left behind—a jagged piece of teakwood lodged between two boulders; a pile of shattered glass in a tidal pool; a section of stainless steel railing that looked as if it had been bent into a crazy pretzel.

Oh, man, Buzz thought. *Pretzels. Burgers. Pizza.*

He couldn't help himself. Only yesterday, they'd had cans of beef stew and ravioli, and one last jar of peanut butter on the boat. Now it was all on the bottom of the ocean somewhere. His belly ached in that way he'd started to recognize here on the island. It was called starving, and not the kind where you missed lunch at school. This felt more like his stomach was eating away at its own empty self, with a sharp, constant pain that left him feeling a little bit dizzy all the time.

Then another unwanted thought pushed its way in. *I don't want to die here.*

He wasn't made for this kind of thing. Not like Carter, or Vanessa, or even Jane. They had their football, and gymnastics, and swimming back home. Jane and Carter had even been camping a bunch of times with their mom.

Not Buzz. He was made for the kind of adventure you enjoyed from the safety of your own couch, with a game controller in one hand and a snack in the other.

Now, if the four of them were going to eat at all,

they were going to have to go out and find the food for themselves. Buzz tried to think of every movie he'd ever seen about this kind of thing, every TV show where some guy volunteered to get dropped off in the middle of nowhere. What did those people eat?

Crabs? Fish? Bugs?

Coconuts!

Of course, Buzz thought. *Duh—coconuts*. It occurred to him just as he spotted several of them washing up and down the beach. They'd probably been knocked loose from the trees by the storm. More importantly, coconuts were something they didn't have to catch, kill, or cook if they wanted to eat them.

Maybe they weren't beef stew, but right now, coconuts were the next best thing.

Island canned goods!

Jane knelt on the floor of the cave, digging through the backpack she'd saved from the boat. There wasn't much inside—they'd had only a minute to grab whatever they could before the boat had been lost.

At the bottom of the pack, she found what she was looking for—Uncle Dexter's journal. It was filled with notes and diary entries for every day he'd ever spent at sea on the *Lucky Star*.

She opened the book to a blank page at the back, picked up one of the two pens she'd managed to save, and began to write.

July 2. Day 8 since we left Hawaii. Day 4 on Nowhere Island.

Huge storm last night. No more boat. No more food. This is everything we have left:

1 backpack
1 journal
2 pens (1 blue, 1 red)
2 blankets
1 pillowcase
1 axe
1 pot
1 big sharp knife

1 regular knife

2 forks

4 spoons

1 plastic bottle (with cap)

6 sea charts

1 rope

1 satellite phone (dead, no charger)

1 laptop (dead)

1 flashlight (broken, but with 2 good batteries)

2 life jackets

"Is that everything?" Jane asked.

Carter and Vanessa were stacking whatever they could find inside the mouth of the cave, where the ground was dry. Almost all of it was covered in mud. The laptop was broken into two pieces now, as if maybe one of the boars had stomped it.

The memory of that stampede, and those crazy screams in the dark, sent a shudder right through her. What if it had been one of them stomped like that? Something like a broken bone out here was almost unthinkable, because what could they do about it? Not much. Not with the nearest hospital a thousand miles away.

"Hey, you guys!"

Jane looked across the clearing to see Buzz coming out of the woods. He had a coil of rope on one shoulder, a shoe sticking out of his pocket, and a plastic soda bottle in his hand. He also had a big green coconut under each arm. She quickly crossed out the number 1s next to "plastic bottle" and "rope" on her list, and changed them both to 2s.

"I got breakfast," Buzz said proudly, dropping it all just inside the cave. "And that's not all."

He reached into another pocket on his cargo shorts and pulled out Jane's camera. Her heart leaped when she saw it. The camera was muddy like everything else, but still in one piece.

"Thank you, thank you, thank you!" She jumped up and threw her arms around Buzz before he could squirm away.

Vanessa was there now, too. She held her hand out for the camera. "Jane, we need to keep that with everything else," she said. "You can't use it for videos anymore."

"What?" Jane asked. "Why not?"

"It's the closest thing we have to a flashlight," Vanessa told her. Her voice softened. "I'm sorry."

Jane wanted to protest. She'd been using the camera to keep careful track of everything they did, before *and* after the shipwreck. If they ever got home again, people were going to want to know about this. It was important. She was dying to turn it on now and make sure her videos were all still there. But Vanessa was right. They couldn't afford to waste the battery.

At home, nobody could have told Jane what to do with her own camera. It was *hers,* after all. Or at least, it had been once. But being on Nowhere Island changed everything. Now that camera didn't belong to her any more than those two coconuts on the ground belonged to Buzz.

The rules were different here.

Carter walked over and picked up one of the coconuts Buzz had brought from the beach. It looked more like a green rugby ball than the brown hairy things he thought of as coconuts back home.

When he shook it next to his ear, a sloshing sound came from inside. That was good news. It meant food *and* drink, all in one. They hadn't had a thing to eat or drink in over twenty-four hours.

"I'll get the axe," he said.

"You want me to do it?" Vanessa asked him.

"I got it."

The axe was his thing. In the first days on the island, it had felt awkward in his hands. But he'd taught himself to choke up for a better swing, just like batting in T-ball when he was a little kid. Soon enough, he'd gotten halfway decent at cutting down palm fronds and tree branches. Hopefully, coconuts would be even easier.

He put his foot up on the first one to steady it and raised the axe blade to his shoulder.

"Careful," Vanessa said.

"I said I've got it," Carter told her.

When he brought the axe down, it split the green hull cleanly down the middle with one satisfying chop. Soon, he was using his fingers to pull the dry, stringy outer husk away from the familiar brown nut inside.

"Save that stuff," Buzz said. "We can use it for making fires."

Carter didn't question it. Jane may have been the bookworm, but Buzz knew more about survival in the wild than any of them. It was kind of funny, since he hardly ever went outside at home.

In a way, Carter felt sorry for Buzz. Everything he knew came from TV and video games, and most of his so-called friends were online geeks just like him. The kid was going to get eaten alive in middle school.

That is, assuming they ever made it off this stupid island.

He set the coconut down again and took another hard swing. But instead of cracking, the exposed brown shell shattered into half a dozen pieces. Before they could even think about saving the liquid inside, it had all spilled into the dirt.

"Carter!" Vanessa said.

"Give me a break," he said. "I've never done this before. I'll get it on the next one."

At least there was still the bright white coconut meat itself. Buzz used a kitchen knife to pry it away from the shell and handed it out piece by piece. The flesh was slimy when Carter tried it, and it didn't taste like much. Still, just to chew and swallow *something* felt amazing.

On the second try, he went more carefully. Once the husk was off, he palmed the coconut and pounded it against the edge of the axe just hard enough to put a crack in the side. It made for sloppy drinking but nobody cared about that. They all sucked down a share of the slightly sweet liquid as fast as they could get it.

"Are there a lot of these on the beach?" Carter asked.

"Some," Buzz said. "Most of them are up in the trees."

"'Cause I'm still starving," Carter said.

Everyone seemed to be thinking the same thing. As much help as the first two coconuts had been, it was a lot of work for just a few mouthfuls.

They were going to have to do better than this.

CHAPTER 3

After their tiny breakfast, Vanessa sat on a fallen tree in the clearing outside the cave. It felt good to soak up some sun at the end of such a long, cold night.

Buzz and Jane flopped on their backs next to her. Carter stayed on his feet, leaning on the axe like a walking stick. Everyone looked exhausted. It was tempting to get some sleep finally, but they couldn't afford to waste the daylight. There was too much to do.

"Listen, you guys," Vanessa said. "We need to start collecting firewood right away. We're going to have to get some water, too, and I think we should—"

"First of all, we need to get one thing straight," Carter said. "You're not in charge here, Vanessa, okay?"

Vanessa glared back at him. Carter had been this way from the moment their parents had introduced the kids to one another. It was as if he was allergic to having anyone else tell him what to do.

"Don't be like that, Carter. We need to make a fire, we need to drink something. And we need to work together," she said.

"That's what I'm talking about," Carter answered. "*Work*. I want to get busy. All you ever want to do is *talk*. I say two of us should go get water while the other two hike up to Lookout Point, grab that signal flare, and bring it down here to make a fire."

"Now who's giving orders?" Vanessa asked. "Besides, we need that flare to stay where it is."

Three days earlier, the four of them had assembled a pyre of kindling and wood to use as a signal fire in case a plane or ship passed by the island. It sat in the highest place they could find, a rocky outcropping above their beach that Jane had named Lookout Point.

In the middle of that pyre, they'd left one of the flares from the *Lucky Star*. The flares were like small, self-igniting torches, but they could be used only once.

"If anyone comes looking for us, we're going to have one chance to get rescued," Vanessa said. "Nothing's more important than that."

"Except staying alive in the meantime," Carter countered. "I was freezing last night, weren't you?"

"I wish we'd taken more of those flares off the boat," Buzz said. "There were at least five of them in the cockpit."

"Yeah, well, I wish we'd taken a lot of things. But we didn't, did we?" Carter asked impatiently.

Vanessa watched Buzz to see what he'd say. Sometimes she wished he'd stand up to Carter more. Besides being the same age, the two boys were nothing alike.

"Vanessa's right. If we can't start that signal fire quick when we need it, then it's not going to do us any good," Buzz said.

But Carter wasn't buying it.

"Once we have a fire down here, we can use it to make a torch or something. We could use that instead of the flare."

"Not if it rains and the fire goes out," Vanessa said. "Besides, do you really think you can get a lit torch all the way up there?"

They'd been back and forth to Lookout Point several times now—up a steep gravel slope, along the narrow lip of a ravine, and across a fallen tree. The idea of trying to do all that with a burning stick in one hand seemed impossible to Vanessa.

"What about you, Jane?" Carter asked. "Do you want to try to sleep through another freezing cold night, or do you want a nice warm fire?"

Jane took a long time to answer. She looked at each of them, as if the gears in her brain were spinning even faster than usual. At home, she was the one who never got into arguments with the others. Jane's mother called her the Great Peacemaker, and said she'd probably win a Nobel Prize one day. Vanessa didn't doubt it.

Still, when Jane finally did answer, it wasn't what Vanessa expected to hear.

"I think we should elect a leader," she said.

As soon as the words came out of her mouth, Jane could feel Carter's glare burning right into her.

"Elect a leader?" he asked.

"Not like a boss," she said. "Just someone who can decide what needs to happen, and how it's going to get done. Like . . . a manager." She knew Carter wanted her to take his side about the flare, but this seemed like the fairest way to decide.

Carter shook his head. "You know what? You've been hanging around these two too much."

"What's that supposed to mean?" Vanessa asked.

"You Diazes are always trying to organize everyone else's life," he told her.

31

"I don't do that," Buzz said quietly, but Carter didn't seem to be listening.

"It's like there has to be a schedule for everything," he went on. "That day we left, your dad made us get to the airport two hours early, just so we could sit around."

"You're the one who never thinks five seconds ahead of time," Vanessa told him. "Someone has to."

"Wrong," Carter said. "*Someone* has to get some water. *Someone* has to build a fire."

Jane hated all the fighting. It was one thing when Carter and Vanessa were at home, locking each other out of the bathroom or seeing who could shout the loudest. But that's not what was at stake here. Why couldn't they see that?

"I'm voting for Buzz!" Jane blurted out. Vanessa and Carter stopped to stare at her. Buzz only looked at the ground, poking the dirt with a long stick. "He knows more about this stuff than any of us."

"You want Buzz to be the leader?" Carter asked. "Don't make me laugh."

Now Buzz did look up. "First of all, I don't want

to be the leader," he said. "And second of all—shut up, Carter."

"You going to make me?" Carter asked.

Jane stood up. "This is what I'm talking about, you guys! I'm the youngest, and even I can see how stupid you're being. Can't we just vote? Please?"

"Fine with me," Vanessa said. "I vote for myself."

"What a shock," Carter said.

"Well, I am the oldest."

"So what? I'm the strongest," Carter said. "I vote for me."

"I vote for Vanessa, too," Buzz said. "And Jane, you should vote for someone else. I don't want it."

"Yeah, Jane. Vote for someone else," Carter said. She could feel that stare of his again, and she knew what it meant. But Vanessa *was* the oldest. She was also way more organized than Carter. That was just a fact.

"Well then . . . I vote for Vanessa," she said softly.

"What?"

"I'm sorry, Carter."

He'd probably expected her to vote for him since

she was his "real" sister. But only Carter thought of it that way anymore. The Bensons and the Diazes were one family now, whether he liked it or not.

"Yeah, okay," Carter said after a long pause. "Vanessa's the leader, but only on one condition. Anyone can change their vote anytime."

"No way," Vanessa said. "That's stupid."

But Carter's hand was already in the air. "This is how we figure stuff out, right? We vote. Jane? Buzz? What do you think?"

"That seems fair," Jane said, and raised her hand. It seemed like a good way for everyone to get something they wanted. "But it has to be three to one. If it's two to two, then nothing changes."

"I can live with that," Carter said.

Buzz seemed to think so, too. "Whatever," he said, and raised his hand. "Can we just get on with this?"

For the first time, Carter sat down. "Yeah, go ahead, Vanessa," he said. "You wanted to be the leader. How are we going to make this fire without a flare?"

Jane held her breath. She knew if Vanessa didn't have some kind of answer, the arguing was just going to start all over again.

But Vanessa didn't even hesitate. She looked right over at Buzz.

"Okay, Buzz," she said. "What do you know about making fire from scratch?"

CHAPTER 4

Buzz knelt in the dirt, feeling ready to collapse, or scream, or both.

In front of him, he had a piece of bamboo, split in half like a long thin bowl. At one end was a ball of coconut husk. In his hand, he held a stick that he'd sharpened with Uncle Dexter's bowie knife. For the last hour, or however long it had been, he'd run the stick back and forth . . . and back and forth. . . . and back and forth . . . over the bamboo, trying to work up enough heat to get the husk to burn. So far, all he'd gotten was a giant blister on his palm and at least a dozen new mosquito bites.

There were other ways to make fire, he knew. They could use eyeglasses to refract the sunlight, if any of them wore glasses. Which they didn't. And there was a bow-and-arrow thing he'd seen on a show once, but the details wouldn't come back to him no matter how hard he tried to remember.

So it was down to this—friction and elbow grease. Buzz just wished he had a little bit more of both. The idea of another long cold night in the dark was almost too much to take.

"Anything?" Carter asked, coming out of the woods with another armload of branches. Behind him, Jane carried a bundle of smaller twigs for kindling. They'd gathered a good amount of firewood by now, but none of it was going to do them any good if they couldn't get a flame going.

"Not yet," Vanessa said.

Buzz sat back, scratching at the bites on his legs. It was impossible *not* to scratch. The mosquitoes were like their own kind of torture up here in the jungle. He'd started to wish for repellent almost as much as food or fire.

Then he felt a tap on his shoulder. "Come on," Carter said. "Let me give it a shot."

He knew this was coming. Carter always had to put himself in the middle of everything.

"I've got it, Carter," he said.

"Do you?" Carter asked, and put his hand out for the stick.

With Vanessa and Jane watching, there wasn't much choice. Fire was more important than anything right now, and the fact was, Carter could outmuscle him at this.

Still, Buzz burned just a little as he handed it over. This was *his* idea, after all.

"Keep the pressure steady," he said. "And keep the stick moving. If it starts to smoke—"

"Yeah, I saw what you were doing," Carter said. He knelt down and started running the stick back and forth with more force than Buzz had been able to muster.

Buzz gritted his teeth. There wasn't anything to say, anyway. If they got fire out of this—great. Nothing else would matter, including who had done it.

In the meantime, he just had to be patient. They all did.

For a long time, Jane watched Carter work in silence. It was hard to tear her eyes away from the stick and bamboo, even without any signs of fire.

Finally, Carter sat back, dripping sweat into the dirt. He looked more than a little annoyed by now.

"You know, it's not like we need four people to do this," he said.

"He's right," Vanessa said. "What we really need is water. Jane, do you think you can get back to the falls if you take the camera for a light?"

Jane knew the question was coming. Besides Carter, she was the only one who knew the way. But she wasn't too excited about it.

Going for water meant heading straight back into the caves. They cut like a huge spiderweb of trails through the island's cliffs and ridges. At the far end of one of those caves was a freshwater falls, the only source of drinking water they'd found so far. With a real flashlight, it might take fifteen minutes to get there. But the camera barely gave enough light to let them take one step at a time. It was going to be a long, slow walk through the dark.

"Buzz, will you come with me?" Jane asked. "I don't want to go alone."

"I don't want you to, either," Vanessa said. "In fact—new rule, you guys. Nobody leaves camp by themselves, okay? It's too dangerous."

While Buzz packed their two plastic bottles into the backpack, Jane went to get the camera. It sat on a little rock shelf at the side of the cave, where Vanessa had organized all of their provisions.

It was reassuring to see the camera's little screen glow to life when she turned it on. The battery wouldn't last forever, but hopefully it would last long enough to get them to the falls and back.

"You ready?" Buzz asked. He had the pack on now, and was peering into the dark ahead of them.

"I guess so," Jane said. It wasn't like they had much choice. She flipped the camera to video mode and pressed Play. The she held it out in front of her to light the way. As they started off, she could hear her own voice coming over the camera's tiny speaker.

"Hi, everyone, this is Jane B, reporting for Evanston Elementary. Today is June twenty-fifth, and it's the first day of our trip. We're just a minute away from setting sail on the Lucky Star.*"*

It was the first video she'd made, Jane remembered. Her own introduction was followed quickly by a second voice that stopped her short not far from the cave entrance. Buzz stopped next to her.

"Bon voyage, my little video artist."

It was her mother. When Jane turned the camera around to see the image, there was Beth Benson. She was standing on the dock in Hawaii with Jane's new dad, Eric Diaz.

"Have a great time," Eric said into the lens. *"And here. Take this for good luck."*

He'd given her the Chicago Cubs hat right off his head. It seemed like forever ago. Now, that cap was somewhere on the bottom of the ocean, along with everything else.

"Go on," her mother said. *"You have to get on board. And sweetie, don't spend the whole time behind that camera. I don't want you to miss out."*

"I won't," Jane heard herself say.

The image on the screen jostled and blurred. The next thing Jane saw was their parents again, as she filmed them from the back of the boat. In the background, Uncle Dexter was ringing a bell.

"Here we go!" he shouted. *"Stand by to set sail!"*

"Have fun!" her mother called.

"See you in a week!" Eric yelled, and the two of them waved like crazy as the image slowly faded to black.

When the video was done, Jane had tears running down her cheeks. It hurt, like an ache in her bones, not knowing when she was going to see her mother again. Not knowing when she was going to get her next hug from Eric.

Vanessa and Carter were there, too. She hadn't even realized they'd come into the cave from outside.

They'd all seen the video, and everyone was crying, including Carter, though he tried to hide it.

"I miss them," Jane said. Even the words were hard to say. "I just want to go home."

"I know. Me, too," Vanessa said, and put her arm around Jane. Both of the boys stayed silent. "But Janie, don't run the video again, okay? Use a still image for the light. It'll eat up less juice that way."

Jane nodded and swallowed hard, trying not to cry anymore. She couldn't afford to be a baby here.

She took a deep breath. "Come on, Buzz," she said. Buzz put a hand on her shoulder, and they set off again, straight back into the darkness.

CHAPTER 5

Time was strange here, Carter thought.

It seemed as if, all of a sudden, half the day was gone and they weren't any closer to having a fire than when they woke up that morning. How was that even possible?

He shook the sweat from his eyes, trying not to lose momentum with the stick. But it wasn't easy, with the blisters on his hands. Or the exhaustion. Every time he slowed down, or stopped to adjust his grip, it was like starting over. The whole thing was getting real old, real fast.

"You want me to take a turn?" Vanessa asked.

"Nope," he said through clenched teeth.

He leaned into the stick, putting his weight behind it as he worked. It made him dizzy, with so little in his belly, but there was no way he was giving up. They *would* have fire before the day was over. That much, Carter promised himself.

For a long time, the only sound in the clearing was the soft scraping of wood on wood, and his own rhythmic breathing. It all kind of blurred together— hand, stick, movement, heat, sweat . . .

And then, almost as if out of nowhere, a little black curl of smoke floated up from the bamboo trough.

"Carter?" Vanessa said.

"I see it."

His heart was already racing, but he ran the stick faster than ever. The muscles in his arm knotted and tensed. His shoulder felt like it wanted to explode. Still, there was no stopping now.

Another few wisps of smoke appeared and curled around one another. This was it! They were actually getting somewhere. Fire meant cooked food, dry clothes, warm nights, enough light to see by. In fact, it meant *everything*. It was the best news they'd had in a week.

"We got it, Nessa," Carter said. "We got it. We got it—"

Vanessa lay flat on the dirt, ready to blow into the husk at the first sign of any flames.

Carter kept going—back and forth.

But the smoke wasn't getting any thicker. In fact, it was doing just the opposite. As suddenly as it had appeared, it started to dwindle. Already, it was down to a single gray thread.

"No, no, no, no, no. . . ."

He gave the stick one last, desperate burst of speed, but it was no good. A few seconds later, the smoke had disappeared completely.

Carter fell back, gasping for breath. A yell of pure rage came up from somewhere deep inside him. He'd never been this frustrated in his life. Not even close.

"That's it!" He hurled the stick into the woods. "I'm getting that flare!"

Vanessa answered quietly but insistently. "No, Carter. We can't. We have to keep trying."

"*You* keep trying," he said, and headed across the clearing for the woods.

"Where do you think you're going?" Vanessa called out, as if she thought being thirteen meant something. They were on their own here. Age didn't matter.

"Where do you think?" he asked.

"Carter—don't!" she shouted.

But he was already pushing through the brush on his way uphill, headed straight for Lookout Point.

"AUUUUUGGGGHHH! GET IT OFF ME! GET IT OFF!"

Buzz's voice echoed off the cave walls, filling his own ears. He ran his fingers furiously back and forth over the spot where *something* had just run its tiny little claws through his hair.

Then another something flitted past his ear with a soft, and eerie, whizzing sound.

He yelled out again and crouched down, covering his head with one hand and waving at the darkness with the other.

Bats. It had to be. He'd been hearing them all along, but now two had just dive-bombed in quick succession.

"Stop moving!" Jane said. She knelt down and held the camera up between them. He could just make out her face in the tiny light. "They're attracted to the motion. It's how they see!"

"I just want out of this stupid cave!" Buzz groaned. "First, it's man-eating pigs, and now this. There're probably rats and tarantulas running around in here, too."

"Probably not tarantulas," Jane said. It wasn't much comfort. "But Buzz, we don't have a choice."

"I know! That's the problem!" he practically shouted back at her. If they weren't all so thirsty, he would have been out of there a long time ago. Not to mention, Carter would never let them hear the end of it if they came back empty-handed.

"Let's just keep moving," Jane said.

But even that wasn't so easy. As they stood up and started walking again, the ground was uneven and hard to navigate. The camera barely gave any light. All Buzz could see as they moved through was the tiny bit of rocky floor in front of Jane's feet.

With a flashlight, or a torch, the cave might have been a very cool place to explore. But not being able to see anything made it creepier than any haunted house. What if there were more boars back here? Could those things see in the dark?

"How much farther?" he asked.

"I think we're about halfway there," Jane said.

He could feel the cavern opening up into a larger chamber around them. Jane had mentioned this part before. There was a pool, or a pond of some kind, straight ahead. They had to walk around it to get to the next section of cave on the way to the falls.

It was tempting to take the water right there, but Buzz knew better. With the sound of a million more bats rustling and squeaking overhead, this pool was just one giant rodent toilet. They'd have to boil the water like crazy to make it safe, and even then, who wanted to drink *that*?

Suddenly, Buzz bumped into Jane. She'd stopped short.

"What is it?" he asked. "I thought we were going to keep moving."

"We were," Jane said. "But this is taking a lot longer than I thought."

"Yeah, and?"

"Well . . . look at this."

She held up the camera to show him. The battery indicator on the little screen had gone from black to flashing red. And that could only mean one thing.

More bad news.

"Carter, stop!"

Vanessa pushed uphill through the woods. Branches slapped at her arms and legs, but she hardly noticed. The important thing was to keep him from getting to that flare.

It wasn't just about Carter getting mad, or striking out on his own. This was about the big picture. If they wasted their only flare, it could threaten their chances of ever getting rescued. And whether Carter liked it or not, *she* was the leader now. Not him.

Soon, she came to the base of the gravel slope that led up toward Lookout Point. Carter was already on his way to the top, scrabbling over the loose gravel and shale. Vanessa took several steps back and got a running start. As she caught up to him, she reached out, but her hand only whiffed off his heel, and she slid back.

"Nice try!" he called out, and kept going.

Everything was a competition to him. His room back home was lined with awards and trophies. But Vanessa had a few trophies of her own. She dug her toes in, lowered her center of gravity, and pushed up the slope as fast as she could.

At the top, a long narrow ridge ran along the edge of a deep ravine. The only way across to Lookout Point was the fallen tree they'd used before. It was an enormous evergreen, and it formed a perfect bridge.

While Vanessa worked her way along the ridge toward the tree, she watched Carter scramble up through its exposed roots, like climbing a crazy ladder, then out onto the trunk.

"Don't do this, Carter!" she yelled.

He didn't even look back. It didn't help that he was so fast, either. By the time she was climbing up onto the tree herself, he was almost all the way across.

It was slower going now. She pulled herself along the trunk, keeping to a low crawl on her hands and knees. One look down to the boulders and scrub brush at the bottom of the ravine, a hundred feet below, was the only reminder she needed. This was no game.

But Carter sure seemed to think it was. He'd reached the far end of the tree now and paused just long enough to look back with a grin. Then he took hold of a sideways branch and swung himself down to the ground like some kind of great ape.

It was a dumb show-off move, and it shook the

entire tree. Vanessa felt the trunk beneath her tremble—and then tilt, just enough to throw her off balance. Both of her legs slipped sideways. Her feet swung wildly in the air. Her mind reeled in a blind rush of panic.

The only thing that stopped her from dropping all the way off the tree was the rutted bark itself. Her fingers dug into it, finding a painful, tentative grip. One quick glance toward the far side of the ravine showed her that Carter was nowhere in sight. He'd already continued on toward Lookout Point, not even realizing the danger he'd left her in.

A second glance—straight down—showed her the rocky ravine floor waiting below. She was alone now. She had to deal with this herself. Somehow.

Vanessa clenched her teeth and squeezed her eyes shut, trying to focus. A vision of Buzz and Jane passed through her mind, like jagged pieces of a broken picture. She had to do this. There was no choice—for Buzz, for Jane, and yes, even for Carter. She couldn't leave them alone here.

Tensing her stomach, and gripping with the last

strength in her arms, she swung one leg up. The tread of her sneaker landed against the side of the tree, and found some purchase there. It wasn't much, but it was enough. With one more hard push, she landed back on top, flat on her belly. Her heart seemed to beat right through the wood.

Starting to move again was an act of sheer will. Vanessa barely even crawled now, dragging herself along the length of the tree instead. When she finally reached the far side, she climbed down to the ground and stood there on shaky legs, trying not to think too hard about what could have happened.

Up ahead, she could see Carter. He was standing near the edge of Lookout Point with his back to her. In his hand, she could see the bright orange cylinder of the flare. He'd already taken it out from inside the signal pyre where they'd stashed it earlier.

But now he was just standing there, doing nothing. It didn't make any sense.

By the time Vanessa caught up to Carter, he still hadn't turned around. In fact, he wasn't paying any attention to her at all. With no trouble, she snatched the flare right out of his hand.

"Carter!" she said. "Do you even know what you just did? I could have fallen—"

But Carter cut her off. He was staring at something off the edge of the point. "Look!" he said, his voice filled with excitement.

Vanessa's eyes flew to the horizon. "What is it?" she said. "A ship? A plane?"

The view from Lookout Point was astounding. The entire ring-shaped island spread out beneath them. It was an atoll, Jane had said, the top of an ancient volcano that had been sinking into the sea over millions of years. You could see where dense green jungle covered most of the land, sloping down toward a shoreline of yellow sandy beaches and black volcanic rock. Behind them, the circular shape of Nowhere Island enclosed an enormous, aqua-blue lagoon. And beyond that was the endless Pacific itself, stretching to the horizon in every single direction.

But Carter wasn't looking into the distance,

Vanessa realized. He was looking almost straight down, toward their beach.

"Carter?" Vanessa asked. "What are you—"

"Just look!" he said, pointing.

There, in the clear blue water just off Dead Man's Shelf, was their boat, the *Lucky Star*. And it wasn't just the boat that made Vanessa's heart leap. It was the thought of everything on board. All the supplies they *thought* they'd lost when the *Lucky Star* was washed away.

Now—maybe, hopefully—it was all back in play.

Jane knew there was no chance she and Buzz could get to the freshwater falls now. With the low battery on her camera, they were going to be lucky to make it back with any light at all.

She'd been this way only once before, traveling in the opposite direction with Carter. And that was with a working camera. Trying to navigate this maze of caverns without it would be impossible. It could even be lethal. Who knew how many wrong turns and dead ends there might be? Or what was hiding in those dead ends?

"We should just fill the bottles here and turn around," Jane said.

She got no argument from Buzz. "It's better than nothing," he said. "Hopefully, they'll have a fire going by the time we get back there and we can boil—"

Jane screamed as something small skittered across her foot.

"What? *What?*" Buzz asked, his own voice filled with panic all over again.

"I thought I felt something," Jane said.

In fact, she *had* felt something. A rat, probably, but it seemed better not to put it into words. Buzz was already freaked out enough. So was she, for that matter. And the longer they stood here, the more the camera was going to run down.

Working quickly, they dipped their bottles into the freezing cold pool and let them fill all the way. Jane tried not to imagine something leaping out at them as she knelt at the water's edge. It was almost as if the darkness itself was alive, and with every passing second she wanted out of that cave a little more.

As soon as they'd screwed the caps on the bottles and zipped them back into the pack, they turned to leave.

"I'll go in front this time if you want," Buzz said. "Keep your hand on my shoulder."

"Thanks," Jane said, handing off the camera. "I'm really glad you're here, Buzz."

It was a relief to let someone else lead. Going first was exhausting. But even so, the camera's red battery indicator felt like a ticking clock, winding down to nothing. If they didn't hurry, they were going to be sorry. And at the same time, the darkness all around them made hurrying almost impossible.

All they could really do now was go one step at a time and hope for the best.

CHAPTER 6

Carter stood on the edge of Lookout Point, staring down at the *Lucky Star*, sitting on the ocean floor. The water was incredibly clear. It was like looking at a picture of their boat through a sheet of glass.

It wasn't too far offshore, either. Once it had washed off the rocks and sunk, it had come to rest on the edge of a coral reef maybe twenty or thirty yards away from Dead Man's Shelf. That meant all the things they thought they'd lost were very possibly within reach—flares, first-aid kit, clothes, blankets, food. It was all just waiting for them down there.

"Let's go," Carter said. "We can do this right now."

"It's getting late," Vanessa said. She pointed west, where the sun was heading for the horizon. "But let's make a deal."

Carter looked her in the eye. The truth was, he didn't totally trust Vanessa. And she probably didn't trust him.

"What kind of deal?" he asked.

She held the flare out on her palm. It didn't look like much, just an orange stick with a black cap, the size of a big Magic Marker. But they both knew that if that cap came off, the flare would burn with the intensity of a blowtorch for a full minute.

"I'll bring this down with us," she said. "We won't use it today, but first thing in the morning, we can dive down to the boat. If we don't find more flares, or figure out some other way to make a fire by this time tomorrow, we'll do it your way. Deal?"

Carter hated the idea of another cold night. But he could be a team player, even if the others didn't think so. Maybe it was time to prove it.

"All right. Deal," he said.

"And listen, Carter. As long as we're talking, can I ask you something?"

"What now?"

"Why are you so mad all the time?" she asked.

It was such a Vanessa question—as in totally unnecessary, Carter thought.

"I'm not mad all the time," he said. "I'm just trying to get stuff done around here, in case you hadn't noticed."

"Is it because you don't like being part of this family?" she asked. "You know, my parents got divorced, too, and you don't see me—"

"Are you serious?" Carter asked. "You really want to talk about that? Right now? Give me a break."

Vanessa took a deep breath and stared at him. "Well, either way, while you're so busy *not* being mad, could you please take it easy on Buzz? He's not as strong as we are."

"He's stronger than you think," Carter told her. "Jane, too. They don't need you to baby them all the time."

"I know," Vanessa said right away. But she wasn't very convincing.

Meanwhile, the sun was going down fast. There wasn't anything else to say, so Vanessa tucked the flare into her pocket and they headed back to camp. First, they recrossed the tree bridge one at a time, crawling carefully to the other side. After that, it was a quick hike the rest of the way down, where they found Buzz and Jane waiting for them at the cave.

Jane was flat on her back, with two bloody knees. Buzz was sitting up, using the big knife to carve a point at the end of a long stick. Both of them looked exhausted and pale.

"The camera's dead," Jane said. "The battery started to run out before we could get to the falls. We had to take water from inside the cave and turn around."

Out by the fire pit, Carter saw two full bottles of water sitting on the ground.

"Are you guys okay?" Vanessa asked.

"We fell a couple of times," Buzz told them. "But we're okay."

While Vanessa gave them the good news about the *Lucky Star*, Carter couldn't wait anymore. He turned and walked back out to where the water was waiting. It didn't make any sense that they'd just leave it by the fire pit, but right now he was too thirsty to care.

He unscrewed the cap on one of the bottles and took a long swig. Then another, and another. It was hard to stop. He couldn't hog it all, he knew, but he could at least have half of a bottle. That was his share. He'd drink it now and go back into the cave for more by himself if he had to.

"CARTER, DON'T!"

Vanessa's voice jarred him out of his thoughts. He almost dropped the precious water right there.

"What?" he asked. "I'm not hogging it."

Something was wrong, he could tell. Jane's eyes were wide.

"We have to boil that first!" she said.

"What do you mean? Why do we have to boil it?" he asked.

"Because," Buzz told him. "You just drank water off the bottom of a giant bat toilet. That's why!"

For the next hour or so, Jane watched Carter carefully. He didn't seem sick, but it was too early to tell.

Then, when Buzz and Vanessa brought four new coconuts up from the beach, Carter said he didn't want his. Instead, he went to lie down on the palm fronds they'd piled into thin mats inside the cave.

That's when Jane started to worry for real.

As it grew dark, the jungle seemed to close in around them. It was like a world of sounds that only got louder as it got darker. Jane could hear a million different insects, and birds, and small animals moving in the underbrush. Somewhere not too far off, a monkey screeched over and over.

It was horrible, knowing exactly how long and cold the hours ahead were going to be, without fire or drinkable water. Carter obviously wasn't well, but what if he got *really* sick? What then?

It didn't take long to find out. It was two to a muddy blanket inside the cave, and he was already shivering when Jane cuddled up next to him.

"Are you going to be okay?" she asked.

"I dunno," he half mumbled. He sounded terrible. And in fact, they'd barely settled in when Carter threw back the blanket and jumped up.

"Which way's the front?" he asked.

"Over there," Jane said. There was just enough moonlight outside to show the way, but he seemed confused. She saw his shadow stumble in the right direction, until somewhere near the cave entrance he threw up for the first time.

But it wouldn't be the last. Not even close.

For hours, Carter vomited, over and over. At first, the little bit of food in his stomach seemed to come up, along with the water he'd drunk. After that, it was just a dry hacking sound that made Jane's own stomach feel queasy.

Her heart ached, too. She wished there was something—anything—she could do to make him feel better.

"I should have told him about the water," Jane whispered to Vanessa and Buzz. "This is all my fault."

"It's not," Vanessa said. "We all should have noticed."

"But I was the one who put it by the fire pit. I should have just held on to it. Or something. I don't know," Jane said.

It was like every small mistake became huge here. There was no doctor to call, no medicine they could give Carter, not even any water to rinse his mouth. The reminders of everything they took for granted at home were endless—like toilets, and medicine cabinets, and electric lights. And parents, who took care of things when it all went wrong. All back in the "real world."

This place felt more unreal every single day.

When Carter finally went quiet, it was almost worse. Jane could just barely see the shape of him in the pale moonlight. He sat slumped over at the far side of the clearing, not moving, or making any sound at all.

"Carter? Are you okay?" she asked.

"Unnnhhh," was all he said back.

She shuffled her feet over the ground, trying not to trip as she went. "I'm coming," she said. She didn't know what she was going to do when she got there, but she couldn't just watch him suffer alone.

Then something else stopped her. At first, it seemed like another sound from the brush, no different than the thousand others. But Jane quickly realized that she was hearing something bigger. Something horribly familiar.

A second later, the heavy shadow of a wild boar came pushing, sniffing, and snorting its way into the camp.

Buzz heard a small scared whine from Jane—just before he looked outside and saw the boar in the moonlight.

At the sight of it, he bolted to his feet. "Jane! Don't move," he called out.

"Are you sure?" she asked, her voice shaking.

In fact, he wasn't sure at all. Could the boar see her? Smell her? Was it about to charge, like the night before? Already, it was moving tentatively in her direction.

Buzz fumbled through the dark now, heading for the pile of gear at the side of the cave.

"Where are you going?" Vanessa asked.

"I'm getting the axe!" he said.

He had no idea whether he could actually use the axe if he had to, but it was a weapon, anyway. He had to do *something*. Jane was so small, and Carter was in no shape for this.

He could hear Vanessa now. She was outside, screaming at the beast.

"Go away! Get out of here!"

Jane was yelling, too, but it wasn't helping. The only answer they got back was a familiar high-pitched squeal.

Buzz fumbled through the supplies. The moonlight did him no good back here. It was like being blind.

"Buzz, hurry!" Jane yelled.

And then he heard Vanessa. "Help!" was all she said. There was a louder snorting sound now, and some kind of shuffling on the ground. Jane screamed again, and Carter yelled out weakly, "Get off her!"

Those three words—*get off her*—sent a cold wave of dread right through Buzz. Where was the axe? Where was it?

"I'm coming!" he shouted.

His hands passed quickly over a life jacket . . . a spoon . . . a shoe . . . and then something small, long, and round. The flare! Of course. The four kids had been shown how to use them, back in Hawaii before they left port. Forever ago, it seemed, but it wasn't a complicated thing.

Another scream from Vanessa sent Buzz running blindly outside. He stumbled over something he couldn't see, but righted himself and kept going. Even as he moved, he held the flare out in front of him and pulled the plastic cap off with a quick, hard jerk.

It exploded to life in his hand like the world's

biggest Fourth of July sparkler. Suddenly, the clearing was filled with a bright white light. Buzz charged straight at the confusion of bodies on the ground. He saw the boar standing over his sister. And he saw Vanessa kicking her legs, trying to roll free.

He yelled as he came closer, thrusting with the burning tip of the flare. The boar turned then, showing him its tusks and teeth, and its tiny wild eyes.

"GET OUT OF HERE!" he shouted. "GO!"

With another squealing scream, it reared off the ground. Vanessa rolled away just in time to avoid being stomped, and the boar bolted into the woods. Buzz followed as far as the tree line, still yelling to drive it off as far as he could. There were other boars, too—a dozen or more of them in the brush. He could hear their hooves drumming the ground as they all retreated through the woods and away from camp.

As soon as the boars were gone, Buzz dropped the flare and ran over to where Vanessa was sitting up. His own breath was still ragged, a combination of terror and trying not to cry.

"Are you okay?" he asked. "Vanessa?"

"I think so," she said.

"Buzz!" Jane yelled. "The flare! The flare!"

"What?" he asked. Her yelling confused him. Was there another boar?

Already Jane was running over to where the flare lay, still sparking on the ground. "We need to start a fire!" she said.

The realization hit Buzz all at once. He'd been too scared to think straight. But this was their chance.

"Go . . . do it!" Vanessa said. "I'm all right!"

He took the flare from Jane and rushed over to the fire pit. The bamboo trough and ball of coconut husk were still there, but no firewood.

"Get some wood out of the cave!" he screamed.

"I can't see!" Jane shouted back. Vanessa was scrambling now, too, and went to help her.

Buzz's hand shook as he bent toward the bamboo. The instant the flare came near the husk, it blazed up brightly and then burned out just as fast.

Meanwhile, the flare itself was starting to sputter and hiccup in his hand. It wouldn't be good for much longer.

"HURRY!" he called. He held the lit end of it to the bamboo now. The little trough glowed orange, and for a few seconds, he felt a glimmer of encouragement. A small flame even licked up from the wood. The edge of the trough blackened as it burned quickly from the last of the flare's power.

"Here! Here!" Jane said. She fell to the ground next to him with an armload of branches. Buzz took several twigs from the pile and stacked them roughly over the bamboo, but there wasn't nearly enough of a flame to get anything going.

The flare was still just barely burning. He shook it in his hand as if that might do any good. A second later, it was dead.

Buzz blinked several times. After the brilliance of the flare, everything seemed even darker than when they'd started. All he could see in front of him was a flat blackness. That was it. There was nothing more they could do until morning.

It was instantly depressing. They'd just lost a real opportunity to get fire. Maybe their only opportunity. The chance had been right there, literally in his hand. And what did they have now? Nothing. They were back to square one.

Not even square one, Buzz realized. Now they didn't even have the flare—the one they'd been saving all along for the most important thing of all.

Rescue.

CHAPTER 7

"**W**e can't stay here anymore," Vanessa said.

It was just getting light out. Somehow, they'd made it through the night without losing their minds. Carter had finally stopped throwing up. He lay on one of the blankets with his arms around his knees, in that half-waking state that had become a part of normal life here.

Buzz had finally found the axe, and it was still in his hands as the sun came up. Vanessa could tell he felt guilty about having used their only flare, but there had been no choice. Just the opposite, in fact. Buzz had saved them.

The only real question was, What now?

"Vanessa's right," Buzz said. "It's too dangerous to sleep up here. Those boars could just keep coming back."

Jane waved at the buzzing cloud around her head. "The bugs aren't nearly so bad down by the beach, either," she said. "And it's not so hot during the day."

The other advantage was that a shelter on the beach would let them keep an eye out for rescue planes and ships, Vanessa thought. That was huge.

For once, everyone seemed to be in agreement. They had to move their camp as soon as possible. But without the cave, they'd be out in the open—in the rain, in the sun. And that brought up the obvious question.

"Anyone know how to build a shelter?" Vanessa asked. "Buzz?"

Her brother shrugged, which she'd come to realize didn't mean no. He was just uncomfortable being in charge of anything.

"I'm not sure," he said. "But there's a lot of

bamboo around. We could make a floor with that. Maybe a roof, too, if we could get a bunch of palm fronds."

"Gee, where are we going to get those?" Vanessa asked. It was supposed to be a joke, but nobody seemed to be in the mood. So instead, she counted off the day's priorities.

"Okay, number one—I really want to try to get down to the *Lucky Star*."

"Me, too," Carter said. "Talk about sunken treasure."

"You should rest," Vanessa told him.

Now it was Carter's turn to shrug. He obviously didn't like being told what to do, even when he was sick. But it wasn't as if he was going anywhere fast that morning. At least he'd had a little coconut water and kept it down. That seemed like a good sign.

"Number two—new shelter," she went on. "Even a lame one could be okay for now, as long as it doesn't rain. And three—we need more coconuts, especially until we can figure out where to get water."

With no flashlight, no camera, and no fire for making torches, there would be no going through the caves to the falls anymore. And even if they could boil the remaining bottle and a half of water from the cavern pool, nobody was prepared to drink it. Not after the night Carter had just had. They'd have to stick to coconut water in the meantime, and keep looking for another source.

"Also," Vanessa said, "number four. There has to be something else we can eat around here."

"There is," Carter said. "Down on the bottom of the ocean. In our boat."

That's not what she'd meant, but he was right about one thing. The *Lucky Star* was exactly where they needed to start.

It took a few hot, sweaty trips to carry all of their things down to the beach, but it was worth it. As soon as Buzz stepped out of the woods, the breeze off the ocean cooled his face. The bugs seemed to go away at the tree line. Even the air was different. Somehow, the jungle smelled like dirt and the beach seemed clean.

They stacked everything they brought under a palm, where the sand gave way to the woods. The rocks of Dead Man's Shelf jutted up on one side here. It all formed a half-sunny, half-shady alcove, where they could make a bamboo lean-to against the rock wall and still keep themselves above the high tide line.

"We should have done this yesterday," Buzz said.

"No time like the present," Jane chirped. Buzz could tell she was glad to get out of the jungle, too. The second run-in with the boars had shaken them all pretty badly.

Meanwhile, there was work to do, and lots of it. Vanessa and Jane were already getting ready to dive down to the boat, while Carter took a minute to catch his breath in the shade.

"We'll just be right over there," Vanessa told him. She pointed up toward the rocks. "Hopefully, this won't take too long."

"I'll cut some bamboo for the shelter," Carter said. "And I can look for more fallen coconuts, too."

"Just rest, Carter. Please?" Vanessa asked. "We can do that when we get back."

There was no question that Carter was too shaky to try to reach the boat. He still looked pale, but Buzz could tell he was trying not to seem weak.

For his part, Buzz was going to help the girls however he could. Diving and swimming weren't exactly his specialty. That was no secret. But given the alternative—hanging out and listening to Carter tell him what to do—Buzz knew exactly where he wanted to be.

"Let's go," Vanessa said, and Buzz followed the girls up onto the rocks, toward the spot where the *Lucky Star* had last been seen.

When Jane first dove into the water, it felt amazing just to rinse off for the first time in days. Jungle living had left all four of them covered in layers of grime. Vanessa's and Buzz's faces were both streaked with dirt as they looked down at her from the rocks above.

"You sure you don't want me to go first?" Vanessa asked.

"I can do it," Jane told her.

It was exciting to think about being the first one to reach the boat. And it couldn't hurt for everyone to stop seeing her as the baby of the family, either. Maybe she was the youngest, but she was a good swimmer. That wasn't being conceited. It was just true.

"It shouldn't be that far," Vanessa said. She pointed straight out from where they stood. "Can you see it?"

Jane ducked her head under the water to look around. Sure enough, there was the *Lucky Star*, a short swim away. It lay half on its side, resting at the edge of a coral reef. Just beyond that, the ocean floor dropped off, farther down than Jane could see. It was like giant underwater stair steps.

"Got it!" she called back. There was no reason

to use up energy treading water, so she started swimming right away.

The ocean was calm this morning. It didn't take long to stroke across its glassy surface, until she was floating directly above the boat. There was the white cabin roof. The pointed bow at the far end. And almost straight down, she could see the cockpit. That's where she needed to go.

According to Buzz, the spare signal flares were in one of the small lockers behind the captain's wheel. Of all the things they wanted to salvage from the boat, nothing was more important than those flares. Especially after the night before. If a ship or plane passed the island now, they'd have no good way of lighting their signal fire up on Lookout Point.

When Jane looked down again, the stainless steel captain's wheel glinted back a few snatches of sunlight from the surface, as if it were showing her the way. She flashed a thumbs-up to Buzz and Vanessa on the shore, then flipped over in the water and started for the bottom.

The salt water stung her eyes as she swam. She kept them open anyway, focusing on the *Lucky Star*. Fish darted in and out of the reef, showing flashes of electric yellow, blue, and even bright pink. The colors got only more intense as she went deeper— but so did the pressure in her head.

It didn't take long to realize this was going to be harder than Jane had thought. The tightness behind her eyes quickly turned into a shooting pain. The urge to turn back was strong.

Just a little farther, she thought. *Just a little farther . . .*

It was a thrill when she reached the boat itself, and touched the edge of the cabin roof. But that was as far as she could go. She turned around and kicked toward the surface, following the trail of her own bubbles.

Her head was pounding as she came up for air. The sunlight seemed to make the headache worse, but she ignored it. She could see Vanessa and Buzz over on the rocks, watching expectantly.

"Anything?" Buzz yelled.

Jane nodded, saving her breath. She wasn't done yet. Before they could tell her to come back, she swallowed another huge gulp of air and headed right back down.

With her arms at her side this time, she found it was quicker to kick all the way, like a dolphin moving through the water. It was only when she reached the boat a second time that she remembered something. It was a trick her mother had shown her, in the pool at the gym back home.

Holding on to the captain's wheel with one hand, Jane pinched her nose closed and blew out. Right away, the pressure in her head eased, with a pop in her ears and a tiny squeaking sound inside her head. She wished she'd thought of it sooner.

Still, she couldn't stay down here forever. Her lungs were already sending up a plea for air. She had to hurry.

Using the spokes of the captain's wheel, she pulled herself down toward the cockpit floor. That's where the three lockers were. The first one was already hanging open. Even through the blur of the water, Jane could make out the empty white space inside. *Nobody home.*

She moved to the second locker and fumbled quickly with the latch. As she pulled the door open, two bright orange floaties popped out in a rush. They shot right right past her and disappeared toward the surface.

The surprise of it forced a gasp of precious air out of Jane's lungs. The need to breathe was becoming intense. Her vision twinkled around the edges, like seeing stars.

No stopping now, though. No way.

She knew if she turned around, she wouldn't be able to make it back down—and then someone else would have to finish what baby Jane had started. Besides, there was just one more locker to check. The flares had to be in there.

It was only when her hand landed on the third locker door that Jane realized it was already ajar. It sent a sinking feeling through her. And sure enough, when she pulled it open, the space inside was just as empty as the first locker had been. If the flares were ever here, they were long gone now.

That was it. There was no more time for thinking. No time for disappointment. Just a desperate need to breathe. The second she realized there was nothing left to find, Jane took off kicking for the surface as fast as she could go.

Buzz tried not to look disappointed when Jane came out of the water empty-handed.

"I don't think those flares are down there," she said. She lay back on the sun-warmed rocks, her chest still heaving as she tried to catch her breath. "Are you sure they were in the cockpit?"

"Pretty sure," Buzz said. "But that was before the whole boat got trashed, so . . ."

There wasn't much to say about that. The flares were probably lost by now.

Jane told them how difficult it had been just getting as far as the cockpit. Reaching the cabin belowdecks was going to be even harder.

"We have to try," Vanessa said. "I'm going to go down."

She didn't wait for an answer. A second later, she dove in and started swimming away from the shore.

While they waited, Buzz looked around at the bits of wreckage strewn on the rocks. If he couldn't dive, maybe he could at least gather some of it and make himself useful that way. The scrap of teakwood he'd seen before was something they could burn, once they had a fire. Or it could be a shelf. Or even a kind of short spear, with its jagged edge where the wood had broken off.

The twisted piece of steel railing didn't look like much, but you never knew. With so little to work with here, there was no such thing as trash. He pulled the steel free, too, and put it with the wood.

The only other nearby thing was a pile of shattered glass. It sat at the bottom of a small tidal pool carved into the rocks. He reached down and carefully took out one of the larger shards, turning it around in the light to see what it might become.

A knife blade, maybe, if he could figure out a way to fasten it to a stick.

The next shard he took out was curved, like a tiny cup. Buzz scooped it back into the water and held it up. It was too small to drink out of, really, and too sharp around the edges.

But then something caught his eye. A small refraction of light was coming through the glass. It showed up as a single white dot, shining on the rocks.

Buzz tilted the little cup, and the dot jumped. It was on his leg now. He left it there, staring at it, while the germ of an idea started to grow.

Sure enough, it wasn't long before the bright white dot started to heat up on his skin.

"Um . . . Jane?" he said.

"Just a second," she said without turning around. Vanessa was just resurfacing, shaking her head no. She hadn't had any luck, either.

"I'm going to try again!" she yelled, and disappeared beneath the water.

Buzz didn't move. He held the glass perfectly

still, even as the heat from the little dot grew into a burning sensation on his knee. He kept it there for as long as he could stand, then moved it away, grinning like crazy.

This wasn't just a piece of glass in his hand. It was a makeshift magnifier—the next best thing to a box of matches out here in the wild.

Maybe it wasn't worth getting *too* excited about. Not yet. But it was also possible that Buzz was going to have some very, very good news to share with the others.

CHAPTER 8

Carter dug his toes into the sand with every step, dragging a long pole of freshly cut bamboo under each arm. When he reached the new campsite, he let them drop next to the four others he'd already harvested with the axe. Then he plopped himself down, lying back and squinting into the bright sun.

He felt empty. That was the word for it. This dizzy, hungry feeling had been bad enough before he got sick. Now it was twice as bad. Just staying upright was a challenge.

Don't stop, Benson. Get up! Keep going!

He'd worked plenty hard before, every day at football practice. Coach Bingham was a maniac, in a good way. *"You boys'll thank me for this."* That's what he'd said so many times it became a joke—but a true one. All Carter wanted to do right now was get up and keep working.

And he would. Just as soon as his head stopped spinning.

"Carter!" Jane called out.

He looked up to see his sister climbing down to the beach from the rocks. The only thing in her hands was a scrap of wood. That seemed like a bad sign, but she was excited about something.

Vanessa and Buzz were close behind. Vanessa had a mangled piece of steel tubing. Whatever Buzz was carrying cupped in his hand, it was too small to see. But he was smiling, too.

"I thought I told you to rest," Vanessa said, looking at the bamboo.

"You did," he said. "And then I remembered that this shelter wasn't going to build itself. So I guess you didn't find the flares, huh?"

"No," Jane said, jumping excitedly from one foot to the other. "That's the bad news."

"What's the good news?"

"This," Buzz said. He held out his hand and showed Carter a few random pieces of broken glass.

"That's the good news?" Carter asked.

Buzz quickly explained his idea. With a little water, some sunlight, and a blank page from Jane's journal, they might actually be able to get a fire going.

"I mean, it's no guarantee," Buzz said, "but—"

"What are we waiting for?" Carter asked. "Let's do this."

Just like everything else, it seemed to take forever before they could actually get started. Buzz dug a shallow fire pit in the dirt while Vanessa and Jane ran up to the cave for a few armloads of wood. It was the one thing they'd left behind, to keep dry just in case of rain.

Carter used the time to open a few of the coconuts he'd gathered so everyone could have something to eat and drink. He set the husk aside, then piled it next to the wood the girls brought down.

Finally, all four of them knelt around the new pit while Jane carefully tore a single white page from the back of her journal. She'd grown as attached to that little book as she'd been to her camera, taking careful notes about everything they did. If they ever got home, she'd probably sell their story for a million dollars, Carter thought. Leave it to Jane.

Buzz built a tiny pyramid of twigs around a ball of coconut husk in the middle of their circle. Vanessa, the only one who had been wearing a jacket on the night they'd abandoned the *Lucky Star,* held her rain slicker up as a windshield. It was much breezier here than it had been up by the cave.

Next, Buzz crumpled up the page from Jane's journal and set it on the ground. He held out the homemade magnifier while Jane squeezed a few drops of water from her long hair, still wet from the ocean.

Finally, he checked over his shoulder for the sun and started tilting the little glass cup back and forth.

"Please let this work," Jane said, in a whisper. "Please, please—"

"There!" Vanessa said, as a speck of white light jumped into view. "Don't lose it!"

"I won't," Buzz answered. His voice was faint, like he was in some kind of trance. The last time Carter had seen him this focused was when he had reached the final level in FarQuest, his favorite game of all time.

Now Buzz was adjusting the glass in tiny, almost imperceptible movements. Slowly, the white light shrank down from a dot to an even smaller pinpoint.

Nobody spoke.

The seconds ticked by, and turned to minutes. Endless minutes. It was almost like time stopped, with everyone frozen in one position.

Even when the tiny spot on the paper finally turned black and started to smoke, Carter didn't let himself get too excited. They'd had smoke before, with the stick and bamboo. All that had gotten him was frustration.

But then, as if out of nowhere, a little yellow

tongue of flame appeared. It popped up from inside the ball of paper, and quickly started to spread.

"YES!" Carter shouted.

"Omigosh!"

"I don't believe it!"

Jane jumped up and hugged him. Even Vanessa hugged him.

This was it. Actual fire! Carter could hardly believe his eyes. The whole idea of getting this far had started to seem so difficult—so *impossible*—that it was almost like looking at some kind of miracle now.

And he hadn't even done it.

Buzz had!

―――

While the others jumped up and started celebrating, Buzz stayed right where he was. He could feel the blood pumping in his ears. It was an amazing feeling, just to get this little flame. But they weren't done yet.

Moving carefully, he pinched the ball of burning paper between his thumb and forefinger. Then he slid it closer to the pile of husk and twigs. Right away, the husk lit up and flamed brightly.

"More husk!" he said. He stuck out his hand like a surgeon on TV, waiting for a scalpel.

Carter grabbed a fistful of the dry stringy material from their reserve and gave it to him. Slowly, Buzz fed it in, bit by bit, as the paper burned down. He blew softly into the base of the fire. He gave it some more husk.

Soon, the smallest twigs started to spark and pop, then burn. Buzz arranged a few more on top of those, and the flames grew a little higher still.

It took some time, but with every step, he could feel a balloon of excitement in his chest, growing bigger . . . and bigger . . . until finally, they had an actual fire blazing in the middle of camp. It was just about the most beautiful thing he'd ever seen.

Vanessa pulled him up off the ground and spun him around in a crazy dance. For a few sweet moments, nobody was hungry anymore. Nobody was miserable. Nobody was even tired. It was as if they'd invented electricity or something.

And nothing had ever made Buzz prouder in his life than this little fire of his, out here in the middle of nowhere, thousands of miles away from the nearest match.

Suddenly, everyone had a whole new energy for the million things that needed doing. They had to gather lots more firewood. More bamboo. More coconuts. More palm fronds.

The shelter—some kind of shelter—had to be built before the sun went down. And the fire would need nonstop tending, like the world's most precious baby. That was going to mean overnight watches, but they'd take turns.

Vanessa didn't put anything to a vote this time. She just thought about who was capable of what and started handing out assignments. If it meant stepping on a few toes, that couldn't be helped.

They were finally getting somewhere.

For her own part, she spent the afternoon hacking at the grove of bamboo they'd found up the beach. There was plenty of it for the shelter, but it was hard work, chopping it all down and hauling it back to camp.

If Carter had been fully well, he probably would have grabbed the axe right out of her hand. Instead, he started cutting palm fronds. Jane picked up the very last of the fallen coconuts, and then switched over to gathering more wood.

Buzz was on fire duty—tending it, watching it, feeding it, and even trying to figure out how to make some kind of torch. Without any flares, a torch might be their only option for lighting the signal fire up on Lookout Point. A torch might also get them through the caves to the freshwater falls. The whole day felt like it was filled with new possibilities.

Besides the fire, Buzz was also the brains behind their new shelter. He wasn't strong enough to hoist the long sections of bamboo by himself, but he did know how the whole thing might come together.

They built the sloped roof first, with a long row of the bamboo poles. Each one had to be shoved into the sand, as deep as possible, and then wedged diagonally up against the wall of their alcove.

Jane came up with the idea of lashing the bamboo together with vines from the jungle, and Carter showed her how to knot them so the thick strands wouldn't come undone.

Finally, as the sun started to drop behind the cliffs, they layered several dozen palm fronds over the top, tucking the leaves in and shoving them between the bamboo to keep them in place.

The whole thing was still pretty shaky. Another big storm would knock it right back down. The roof wouldn't keep out much rain either, and they still needed a floor.

But it was a start. A great one, in fact—made even better by their brand-new fire.

As Vanessa sat there that evening, slowly chewing her coconut, she was as close to comfortable as she'd been since they'd gotten to Nowhere Island. Watching the flames dance, and thinking about the light and warmth they were going to give through the night, she felt as if she and Buzz and Carter and Jane were finally coming back to life.

I'm not the same person anymore, she thought.

It wasn't exactly a news flash, but the realization was a sudden one all the same. She'd made it through a shipwreck. She'd lived for nearly a week on next to nothing. She'd *survived.*

Before all this, her most prized possession in the world was the diamond pendant her father and Beth had given her on their wedding day. Now nothing meant more than that little curved piece of glass, tucked away between the rocks for safekeeping. Anywhere else and it would have been a piece of garbage—something to be thrown away. But here, it was going to help keep them alive.

If she ever made it home again, Vanessa thought, she wasn't going to be the same girl who had gotten on that sailboat in Hawaii nine days ago. That much was clear. Something inside her had definitely changed.

Or maybe everything had.

CHAPTER 9

When Buzz woke up the next morning, he was relieved to smell the fire. It was still going.

He'd taken the first watch of the night. Then Carter had spelled him, and Vanessa had taken the last shift. When Buzz crawled out of the lean-to, he could see her sitting on a log by the fire, with her arms pulled inside her shirt against the chilly morning air.

"Where's Carter?" he asked.

"He's cutting more bamboo," Vanessa told him. "We need a floor for that shelter."

"I hear that," Buzz said.

They'd laid a few fronds on the sand the night before, but several new pests had quickly found them. Small crabs had skittered over their bodies in the dark, and some kind of tiny insect had crawled in Buzz's ears and up his sleeves and shorts through the night. Now he was itching in all kinds of new places. He'd also seen at least a few rats sneaking around. The idea of getting off the ground while they slept seemed like a great idea.

So did catching those crabs. Or even a rat. He was *that* hungry.

"So I guess Carter's feeling better?" Buzz asked.

As if on cue, Carter's voice broke the morning air.

"I'm staaaaarving!" he said, walking into camp. He had two more pieces of bamboo trailing behind him. His hair was dripping, and his shirt was off. It looked as if he'd taken a morning swim.

"I've got an idea about how to get some of those coconuts down from the trees," he said. "I'm going to need Jane, one of the ropes, the big knife, and the rain slicker."

"The rain slicker?" Buzz asked. The idea of Carter wearing Vanessa's bright green jacket was kind of funny, but it also didn't make sense. The sky that morning was just as cloudless as it had been the day before.

"Come on, Jane," Carter said, poking his head into the shelter. "Let's go do this."

Meanwhile, Buzz had a few ideas of his own.

"I was thinking we could try to spear some crab or fish," he said. "And I know this is gross, but I saw a ton of snails on the rocks yesterday."

"Eww!" Jane stuck her head out of the shelter, looking horrified. "Are you serious?"

"You don't have to eat them," Buzz said. "But technically, they're meat."

"Yeah. Snail meat," she said.

"New rule," Vanessa said. "No whining."

"New rule," Carter said. "No more rules."

"I'm not whining," Jane protested. "It's just gross. That's a fact."

"What about the fish?" Vanessa asked Buzz.

Buzz shrugged. "We can try." He picked up the big knife and the long stick he'd been working on, then started shaving down the tip. It was like sharpening a giant pencil.

"Buzz, I need that knife," Carter said. He already had the rope and the slicker over his arm.

"Just a second," Buzz said.

"Do want me to get the coconut or not?" Carter demanded. He glared down at Buzz with his hand out. Buzz just stared back, and for several seconds, neither of them budged.

But then Buzz blinked and looked away. "Fine," he said, and dropped the knife for Carter to pick up. "I'm done with it anyway."

It was embarrassing—and infuriating. Buzz *always* looked away first. It was as if Carter was made of stone. One of these days, his new brother was going to push him too far. And then . . .

Well, Buzz thought, he had no idea *what then*. The fact was, he couldn't compete with Carter. He wasn't as strong, or as confident. He'd never even been in a real fight before.

But then again, Buzz thought, everyone had their breaking point.

Didn't they?

<hr/>

After a quick scout up and down the beach, Carter stood with Jane at the base of the shortest palm tree he could find. The bundle of green coconuts he'd been eyeing was at least twenty-five feet over their heads.

"What are we doing?" Jane asked.

"I'm going to get you up there," he told her. "Stand up with your arms out."

Jane had been sitting in the sand, writing in her journal. Now she got up and stood, making a T with her arms.

Carter slipped an end of rope through one sleeve of Vanessa's slicker and back out the other. Then he held the coat up for Jane to put on.

It was the bosun chair on the *Lucky Star* that had given him this idea. When they were sailing with

Uncle Dexter, Carter had ridden straight up the mast wearing the special harness. It raised him fifty feet off the deck, just to change a lightbulb. It had also been the coolest ride of his life.

Now he looked at Jane in the rain slicker with the rope hanging out of her sleeves, and he tried to remember how the harness had held his arms and legs.

Once he'd zipped her in, he wound the rope in a figure eight several times around her shoulders, then her middle, and finally her legs. When it was done, he tied it off with a nautical knot that Uncle Dexter had taught him. Dex called it a Benson special, after Carter. The knot probably had some old seaman's name, too.

"You okay?" he asked.

"Sure. What next?" Jane said.

Carter picked up the opposite end of the rope and tied it to the craggy black rock he'd picked off the beach. It was big enough to have some weight, but small enough to throw.

Now he eyeballed the tree. Leaning back on one

foot, he threw the rock straight up into the crown of greenery at the top, while the excess rope trailed behind. The rock whiffed a low-hanging frond and fell back down into the sand.

"A swing and a miss," Carter said.

"Try again," Jane told him.

This time, the rock got stuck in the foliage. Carter had to yank it free. "Don't give up!" Jane encouraged. Then he threw again. And again. And again. It was like some kind of endless carnival game.

Jane kept track, of course. On the eighteenth throw, he finally hooked the rope up and over one of the tree's big fronds.

"Yes!" Jane said, applauding.

He shimmied the rope back and forth, nestling it into the crook between the limb and the tree trunk itself. Then he pulled hard on both ends of the line to make sure it was strong enough. It was like a big pulley, with Jane at one end of the line.

"All right, Jane. You're up," he said, and handed her the big knife. Jane had already wrapped it in a thick leaf from the woods. She tucked the sheathed blade into the rope around her middle and gave Carter a thumbs-up.

"Ready," she said.

Carter got a good grip on the line and started hauling Jane into the air. She scrambled a little as she rose, but quickly found her balance, pressing her bare feet against the trunk. It was like watching her walk up the side of the tree.

"I've got you!" he said, pulling her higher, hand over hand on the rope. That part wasn't hard. Jane weighed about half an ounce compared to him.

When she reached the top, she grabbed hold of the nearest limb and scrambled up inside, like some kind of baby bird crawling into its nest.

"Jane?" Carter yelled. There was no more tension on the rope, and he couldn't see her at all. She'd just disappeared. "Jane!"

"I've got it!" she called back.

She popped out then, leaning down through the greenery, knife in hand. From there, she started sawing away at the stem holding the coconuts to the tree.

"Mom would kill me if she could see this," Carter said.

"Probably," Jane said. "But it's okay, Carter. I'm fine."

She sawed a little harder, and the bundle of coconuts broke halfway free—but so did the limb that was holding most of Jane's weight.

"JANE!"

For a split second, she fell. On instinct, Carter dropped to the sand, sitting down hard to take up the slack in the rope. Jane jerked to a stop, bounced once, and stayed where she was. The frond above her was at a crazy angle, but it still seemed to hold her weight.

"I'm going to bring you down! Just hang on," he said.

"Don't!" she said. "I've almost got it."

It was typical. Jane was afraid of eating snails, but not hanging upside down, twenty-five feet in the air, on a homemade harness. She even let out a giggle.

"Stop laughing. You gave me a heart attack!" he yelled.

"I know. That's why I'm laughing," Jane said. "Just hang on."

She reached up, folding herself in half to get at the coconuts one more time. Carter braced himself, ready to catch her if he had to. But with a few quick strokes of the knife, the coconuts pulled free.

"Breakfast, lunch, and dinner, coming down," Jane yelled, just as they thudded into the sand.

Their mother would have definitely killed Carter if she could see this, Carter thought. *No question.* But she might have also thought Jane was just as amazing as he did right now.

Vanessa used a spoon to pry another snail off a rock and dropped it into the pot. Buzz had been right. There were hundreds of them along the shore, if not thousands, each one about the size of her fingertip. Inside every half-open shell, she could see a slimy little black and white piece of snail. Also known as protein.

So far neither of them had tried eating one of the snails raw. Vanessa knew people ate them somewhere in the world. Maybe in France. But she was pretty sure those were cooked. For now, she could hold on until they got back to camp, where they could boil or fry them.

While Vanessa worked around the rocks, Buzz stood up to his knees in the ocean with his handmade fishing spear. He'd made several throws with it, but hadn't come up with anything so far.

Before that, he'd tried chasing down the crabs on the beach. That hadn't gone too well, either. It looked as if lunch was going to be snails and whatever coconuts Carter and Jane were able to get.

As she worked, Vanessa also kept her eyes moving, all the time. She looked back toward camp to make sure the fire was still burning. She watched the horizon for any signs of rescue. And she also peered several times up the rocky shore that extended away from their beach.

"What do you think is over that way?" she asked.

"I don't know," Buzz said, sounding distracted. He stood perfectly still in the water, waiting for another fish to go by. "More cliffs, I guess."

It was one of the few parts of the island they hadn't explored yet. So far, it hadn't seemed worth trying. The black volcanic rocks were rough to the touch, and even sharp in some places. You could lose a lot of skin if you went down hard.

All at once, Buzz hurled the spear. It made a small splash and floated away in the direction he'd thrown it. He cursed under his breath as he ran to pick it up again.

"You want to pick snails?" Vanessa asked. "Maybe Carter could try that spear later—"

"I can do it!" he snapped. When she looked down, his face was red, and not just from the sun. "We don't need Carter for everything, okay?"

"I didn't say that, Buzz. I just said—"

"Yeah, I heard you the first time," he said.

Vanessa took a deep breath. "Fine. Keep trying," she told him, and turned away. She dropped another few snails into the pot. Checked the fire. Looked at the horizon. And then she looked up along the rocky part of the shore again.

A few days earlier, Jane and Carter had gone more than halfway around the island in the opposite direction, searching for water. The high tide had trapped them on that side overnight. Ever since, they'd all been reluctant to wander too far.

Still, Vanessa thought, she would have given anything for an hour of privacy right about now. Never mind having a bedroom with a door and a lock. Or a hot shower. Or a simple conversation with someone her own age. Just to have some space, where she didn't have to worry about what everyone else was doing, or what they were going to eat—or, for that matter, where she wasn't getting yelled at for trying to help. . . .

Right now, that sounded a whole lot like heaven.

CHAPTER 10

Jane sat with her back against the shelter wall, trying to stay out of the breeze. The wind had definitely kicked up this afternoon. Looking out at the ocean, she could see small whitecaps where the waves were breaking, maybe a hundred yards offshore. If they were going back down to the *Lucky Star,* she thought, they should probably go soon.

While she waited for the others to get ready, she opened the journal on her lap to a new page at the back. She pulled one of her pens out from the crevice in the rocks where she'd stashed it. And she started to write.

July 4. Day 10 since we left Hawaii. Day 6 on Nowhere Island.

I can't believe it. We've been here for six days! It feels like forever, but it also feels like we just got here.

We're missing the Fourth of July, too. I keep thinking about the fireworks back home, and wondering what Amelia and Becca are doing. Also hot dogs, popcorn, chocolate-chip milkshakes, and food, food, FOOD!

Speaking of food, guess what I ate today? SNAILS. It was Buzz's idea. Once you cook them, they get all tough, but I still don't really know what they taste like. The best way to eat them is to hold your breath and swallow without chewing. And even then—HORRIBLE. Snails are my new most-hated thing about being here.

It also takes FOREVER to get them ready. We spent practically half the day using rocks to crack open these teeny-tiny shells and then taking out the snails inside to cook in the pot with water from the ocean. Now everything smells like SNAILS SNAILS SNAILS.

Vanessa, Buzz, and Carter keep talking about fishing, or catching crabs, but so far nobody knows how to do it. What we need is a fishing pole, or a net, or SOMETHING. Fingers crossed that we can figure it out because here is everything we've had to eat and drink in the last THREE DAYS:

Water

Coconut water

Coconut meat

Snails

Later, we're going to try to get down to the Lucky Star again. Buzz said he had an idea about it. Hopefully, the next time I write something, I'll have some GOOD news to share for a change.

Fingers crossed. (Toes, too!)

Buzz carried one of the ropes up onto Dead Man's Shelf that afternoon. It was a simple enough idea for reaching the *Lucky Star*. As for whether or not this would work, it was like everything else. The only way to find out was by trying.

"First, someone swims down and ties it to the rail on the boat," he told the others. "Then the next person can use it to get down there. Hopefully, you can pull yourself faster than you can swim."

"Like an underwater zip line," Jane said. "Cool."

"That means extra time to get inside the cabin," Vanessa added. "I like it."

Jane volunteered to swim down first and tie off the rope. She slipped easily into the water, carrying one end with her while Carter held the other end on the rocks. Buzz watched carefully as the rope unspooled, making sure it didn't get tangled. The ocean wasn't as calm today. The wind was creating a choppy current that might slow them down. Then again, it might make the rope that much more useful.

It didn't take long to find out. Within a minute, Jane was back at the surface, smiling up at them. "I did it!" she said, climbing onto the rocks. "I think this might work."

When Buzz pulled up the slack, the line was nice and secure. But the boat itself seemed to be shifting with the current—just enough to pull and give, then pull and give again on the rope. It was going to be tricky, but not impossible, for one of them to keep it taut up top while someone else dove down.

"Who's next?" he asked.

Carter had his shirt, shoes, and socks off before there could be any argument.

"Are you sure you feel okay?" Vanessa asked him. His only answer was to dive into the water and take hold of the line.

"Wait!" Jane called. She handed him the empty backpack they'd brought from camp. "Bring back something good."

"You got it, Janie," he said.

"Don't try to grab everything on the first time," Vanessa said. "Just do what you can."

"I always do," Carter said with a grin. "Benson's on the job."

He had a familiar cocky look in his eye. Buzz had seen it before. It was Carter's game face—the one he wore most of the time. Or at least, anytime he wanted to *win* something.

Buzz hoped so, anyway. Because this time, if Carter won, they all won.

Carter took three deep breaths, in and out. On the third breath, he held it, grabbed hold of the line, and started pulling himself down toward the boat.

Buzz's idea actually worked pretty well. He skimmed through the water much faster than he could have swum it. It got him down to the *Lucky Star* in less than half a minute.

The boat sat perched near the edge of a steep drop-off. Beyond that, all Carter could see was open blue ocean. He could hear a muted groan, too. It was coming from the *Lucky Star* as it shifted and listed there on the coral ledge.

Carter stopped long enough to squeeze his nose and release the pressure in his head, then kept going.

Moving quickly, he swam down the galley stairway and into the cabin belowdecks. It was bizarre, swimming through this space where they'd lived for four days before the shipwreck—and three days after. Now the inside of the cabin was more like a giant aquarium. A small school of fish darted out through the opposite hatch as Carter came in.

The fish could have it, he thought. Just as long as they left the canned goods alone.

He turned one-eighty at the bottom of the stairs and went straight for the cooking area in the galley. Everything was even more wrecked than the last time he'd seen it. Most of the cabinets sat at odd angles where they'd pulled away from the walls. Several drawers lay smashed on the floor. Carter started opening whatever compartment doors he could get to, feeling around inside for any signs of food.

In no time at all, it seemed, his lungs started to tighten up and beg for air. He tried to ignore the feeling. He kept his body moving through the water, his hands reaching for the next cabinet door.

It was on the cabinet farthest from the galley entrance that he hit the jackpot. As he reached into a dark corner, his hand landed on something smooth and cool. When he pulled it out, he saw it was a can of some kind. The label had already washed off, but it didn't even matter what was inside. This was real food! Their first in days.

He shoved the can into his pack and quickly swam back outside. When he reached the rope again, he started pulling himself toward the surface as fast as he could go. The need to breathe was everything now. The best he could do was distract himself with a play-by-play inside his head.

Benson's got the ball . . . he's past the sixty-yard line . . . the fifty . . . the forty . . .

His throat pulsed, trying to force new air down

into his lungs. His vision swirled, but the white-bright light at the surface showed him which way to go. It wasn't even the sky he saw. It was the lights of Soldier Field, egging him on.

He's passing the thirty . . . the twenty . . . the ten . . . he's got this!

Carter broke the surface like a shot, and gasped a desperate, much-needed lungful of air before he pulled out the silver can and held it over his head with a yell.

"And Benson scooooores!"

CHAPTER 11

For an hour or more, Carter, Vanessa, and Jane took turns diving down to the boat. It was a slow, methodical process. By the time any of them got inside the cabin, it didn't leave much air in their lungs for rooting around and pulling out supplies.

Still, the salvage pile grew, bit by bit. Vanessa brought up two more blankets from the sleeping cabins. Jane grabbed a pillow on each of her two trips down. Carter found a second can of food and another sharp knife.

A new cooking pot came up. Two pairs of socks. A screwdriver. Three more rain slickers.

But it couldn't go on forever. As the time passed, the day grew windier. The current picked up as well, and each dive was a little more difficult than the one before. Every time the *Lucky Star* shifted, it pulled a little harder on the rope, and there was another low-pitched groan, or a sharp crack from the breaking hull. It was as if the whole boat was threatening to collapse on itself at any moment. They were going to have to stop soon.

Then, on his fifth dive down, Carter found something he'd almost given up thinking about.

After raiding the galley and sleeping cabins, he'd turned his attention to the storage compartments under the navigation desk. One of the cockeyed panel doors was stuck closed, but he wedged his heels against the wall and pulled, breaking the door right off its hinges.

As his eyes adjusted to the dark inside the compartment, a flash of orange caught Carter's eye. And then he realized what he was looking at: a signal flare, floating in the far back corner, just out of reach.

This was huge. Flares were nearly as valuable as

food, if not more. He knew he had to get it somehow.

But he also knew he was going to need a second wind before he could finish. Reluctantly, he turned away, swam up through the galley's hatchway, and hurried back toward the surface.

As he pulled himself along the rope, Carter heard another groan from the *Lucky Star* behind him. It shifted harder than ever, with a strong tug on the line. At the same time, a splash came from up top, and he saw Vanessa fall into the water. It looked as if the pull on the rope had dragged her right off the rocks where she'd been holding the line.

"That's it," she said as soon as Carter was there. "This is getting too dangerous. We have to stop."

"Not yet," Carter said. "There's a flare down there. We have to get it."

He quickly spotted a forked branch among the rocks and picked it up. Hopefully, it would be enough to hook the flare.

"Carter, you're spent," Vanessa said. "I can tell just by looking at you."

It was true. The excitement of pulling the new

supplies out of the boat had carried him this far, but he could feel the toll it had taken on his body. His muscles were like rubber—but his mind was still willing. That would have to be enough for now.

"One more trip," he said. "It'll be worth it. I promise."

Vanessa didn't argue. The fact was, they needed that flare. It was the one sure way to light their signal fire on Lookout Point.

Before there could be any more conversation, Carter got back in the water and headed down. He knew he had to hurry.

As soon as he was back inside the boat's cabin, he went straight for the open compartment under the nav station. The flare was still floating there—and still just out of reach. He had to press his arm inside, all the way up to the shoulder, and cast around with the stick he'd brought down. His back scraped hard against the compartment's broken hinge, but he ignored the pain. There was no time to worry about that.

As he worked, the *Lucky Star* shifted again. A

loud grinding sound came up from underneath. The woodwork around him cracked and popped. It felt as if the whole boat was being dragged by the current, across the rock and coral ledge outside.

Carter knew he had to go. *Right now,* his mind screamed. But another part of him answered back just as clearly: *Not without that flare!* He pushed hard against the compartment opening, willing his arm to stretch another inch or two.

And then he felt it—a slight drag on the stick as it caught something. He dropped the branch now, and snatched blindly for the flare. A second later, his fingers closed around it. Even with his air running out, the adrenaline of the catch was a sweet feeling.

But before he could turn to leave, the boat took one more turn for the worse. Another heavy scraping sound came up from below. The *Lucky Star* tilted, and a rush of seawater flowed through the cabin. The whole craft seemed to have reached the very edge of the coral shelf where it sat.

And now it was going over.

Carter yanked his arm free of the compartment.

His hand scraped hard across the broken hinge. He felt a sharp flash of pain and saw a cloud of his own blood in the water, but that was the least of his worries. He kept a tight grip on the flare, even as the boat continued its unstoppable slide.

Everything was moving now. The cabin itself turned a full ninety degrees around him. The bow rose up, and the *Lucky Star* went vertical in the water.

Carter struggled against the current running through the boat. He stroked as hard as he could—swimming *up,* through the cabin—toward the hatchway over his head. At the same time, the boat slid in the opposite direction. The hatch rushed at him, faster than he expected, and the edge of it caught him hard on the shoulder.

More than anything, he needed *out.* He could feel himself sinking, right along with the boat. The pressure in his head was building, stronger than ever, and there was no time to clear it.

He was so close—he could see outside the cabin, but his muscles were past the point of exhaustion.

Still, failure was no option. He twisted his body halfway around, trying to align himself with the hatch. A second later, he managed to move up and through it with several hard fluttering kicks—out into the open water at last.

A quick glance over his shoulder gave Carter the last view of the *Lucky Star* he'd ever have. It fell away behind him, off the coral ledge and down toward the ocean floor beyond. There was still a powerful downward pull in the water, but no more groaning, no more cracking. Everything went weirdly silent, as his lungs sent up a frantic plea for air. His head was pounding like a drum, and his body was spent.

But most of all, that bright orange flare was still in his hand. He'd promised himself he wouldn't come back without it—and he hadn't. Do-overs didn't come easily in a place like this, Carter thought as he kicked toward the surface. And he'd just scored a big one.

Mission accomplished!

CHAPTER 12

Buzz didn't even know anything was wrong until he saw the blood dripping off Carter's hand.

"It's okay," Carter kept saying as they climbed down from Dead Man's Shelf. "I'm fine, I'm fine."

Jane seemed the most upset. She made Carter sit still long enough to let them look at the cut, while Buzz heard about what had happened with the *Lucky Star*.

That was it, then. The boat was gone. Whatever they'd salvaged was all they were going to get. But at least they had the new flare, along with the two cans of food and everything else.

Carter had sliced the side of his hand, from the base of his pinkie finger down to his wrist. The cut was long, but shallow. At home, it wouldn't have been a big deal at all. Here, it was more of a concern.

"You need to keep that clean," Buzz told Carter. "It could get infected."

"It'll be okay," he said, pulling his hand away.

"Yeah, well, we just need to make sure it stays that way," Vanessa said.

The closest thing they had to bandages were the new socks from the boat. As soon as they were dry, Buzz thought, they could cut the toes off one and make a kind of fingerless glove for Carter to slide on. Anything to keep the cut covered up. But then again, Carter would probably never go for that.

In the meantime, everyone else's attention had turned to the two silver cans they'd brought up from the boat. Vanessa insisted that they eat only one now and save the other. Still, Buzz could feel the mood in camp shooting sky high. Anything to eat besides coconut and snails was worth celebrating.

Carter held the two cans up, one in each hand.

"Pick one, Jane," he said. Jane's eyes lit up, and she tapped the one on the right.

"I'll get the big knife," Vanessa said.

It was ravioli, as it turned out. They didn't bother heating it over the fire. They just passed the can and a spoon around the circle, taking turns. Even so, it was the most amazingly delicious thing Buzz had ever eaten in his life. He'd never known food could taste this good.

Each of them got three and a half ravioli, plus several scrapes with the spoon to gather up every last bit of sauce that clung to the side of the can. It didn't fill their bellies, or even come close, but it was more than they'd had in three days.

Once the can was empty, everyone got busy again. Carter insisted on taking the new flare up to Lookout Point himself, to store it inside the signal fire where the last one had been.

"I want to do a test run," he said. "See how fast I can get up there, just in case."

It wasn't a bad idea, actually—and none of them was faster than Carter. That was just a fact.

Jane said she'd go, too. And take notes, of course.

Buzz and Vanessa stayed back at camp, taking care of the new supplies—spreading out the blankets, pillows, jackets, and socks in the late-afternoon sun. With any luck, everything would be dry in time for sleeping that night. Just the idea of having his own blanket was exciting, Buzz thought.

It wasn't exactly Christmas, but it *had* been a pretty good day. For Nowhere Island, anyway.

July 4 (part 2). Day 10 since we left Hawaii. Day 6 on Nowhere Island.

You know what's better than snails? RAVIOLI! We just ate a whole can of it, split four ways. I think it was the best thing I ever tasted in my life!

After that, we took a practice run up to Lookout Point. That's what Carter called it. We don't have a stopwatch, but we're guessing it took six minutes.

Carter says if he keeps trying, he can get his time down. Maybe to five minutes. Or even four and a half. Because if a boat or a plane comes looking for us, we need to get up there and light that signal fire ASAP!!!

We'll try again tomorrow. It's been a super-long day and everyone's really tired. In fact, I'm going to sleep right now. GOOD NIGHT!

141

CHAPTER 13

Vanessa took the first shift that night, watching the campfire. While the others slept, she pulled out the sea charts they'd saved from the boat and tried to read them by firelight. It wasn't easy. Most of the charts looked alike. So far, the closest they'd come to figuring out their location was a triangle of ocean, fifteen hundred miles on each side.

But maybe there was still some kind of answer here—any clue at all about what they should do next.

For the last three days, it had been impossible to think about anything beyond food, fire, and staying alive. The Coast Guard was out looking for them, that much they knew. But it was no guarantee. If they didn't do everything they could to try to save themselves, they might very well regret it in the end.

Eventually, she put down the charts and picked up Jane's journal. Before Jane took over the book, Uncle Dexter had filled its pages with entries about his different sailing trips. There were notes about weather and navigation, cloud formations and wildlife—but there didn't seem to be anything they could really use.

She wasn't giving up, though. She couldn't. So she turned to page one and started reading all over again.

As the night wore on, Vanessa's head drooped, and she jerked awake more than once. Each time, she threw extra wood on the fire and pulled up closer where the light was better. Still, her eyelids seem to get heavier no matter what she did.

The next time she snapped awake, Vanessa sensed right away that something was wrong.

Looking down, she realized her lap was empty. Not only that, but something was blazing up extra brightly in the fire.

Jane's journal! The open pages were in flames, blackened and curling at the edges. A good part of the book had already been destroyed.

Vanessa jumped up, looking around for a stick or anything to pull it out of the fire. The first thing she spotted was Buzz's fishing spear. She snatched it up, hooked the tip under the journal, and gave the whole thing a fast, hard flick. By the time she'd realized her own mistake, it was too late. The flaming book arced up and out of the fire, then landed on the dry fronds that covered the shelter just a few feet away.

"NO!" Vanessa screamed.

It all went up faster than she would have thought possible. The fronds had been drying in the sun all day and couldn't have been more flammable. With amazing speed, the fire jumped from one section of roof to the next, until the whole top of the shelter was in flames.

"Jane! Buzz! Carter!" she screamed. "Get out of there!"

She heard Buzz yell as he emerged from the lean-to, dragging a blanket and pillow behind him.

"Jane, wake up!" Carter shouted. Vanessa looked in to see him scooping her into his arms, and they rolled out onto the sand, where Buzz was there to help them get away. The flames themselves were falling like huge drops of fire onto the newly laid floor of the shelter. Vanessa managed to pull out two more blankets before it was too late. Already, the palm mats where they'd been sleeping had begun to burn.

"Stay back!" she screamed. She picked up the two cooking pots on the fly and raced down to the ocean. Buzz was right behind with the two plastic bottles. Carter and Jane were there now, too, tearing off the rain jackets they had been sleeping in and scooping them into the waves for any amount of water the material might allow them to carry back.

Vanessa's breath seared her lungs as she tore back toward the shelter. The fire illuminated the whole beach now—it was an incredible sight. Large embers from the paper-thin palms floated on the updraft, like red-orange wings.

Even as she threw her pitiful amount of water at the fire, she looked up to see the tree above her starting to burn. Several dead brown fronds lit up just as easily as the ones on the shelter, until the tree itself was like a giant torch. There was nothing they could do about that. She turned and ran back to the shore to refill the pot.

They made trip after trip to the ocean, barely even speaking as they threw whatever water they could onto the blaze. The sand and rock around the shelter seemed to do as much as anything to keep it contained. Mostly, they had no choice but to let the whole thing run its course.

Slowly, the flames died out, and the whole shelter started to smoke and sizzle. The green bamboo had been slower to ignite, and still showed them the basic structure they'd built, like a charred black shadow of its former self. After working so hard to get the lean-to built, the fire had stolen it away from them with stunning swiftness.

For a long time, nobody said a word. Jane and Carter huddled together in a blanket, while Jane sobbed. Clearly, she was heartbroken about the journal. Everything in it was lost. That included all of Dexter's old notes, Vanessa realized. Whether or not the book had held any secrets for them, they'd never know now.

Already, Buzz was using one of the pots to scoop orange embers into a pile. He poured them together in the fire pit, trying to get a campfire going again. Even now, that was something they had to worry about. Always, always, always.

On top of that, Vanessa noticed, none of the others were even looking at her. It was as if they couldn't bring themselves to meet her gaze or say a word. And she couldn't blame them, either. This was all her fault.

After a while, she stumbled away from camp and sank down on the beach, her mind reeling. How could this happen, on top of everything else? What were they doing wrong? What was *she* doing wrong?

How could she have made such a stupid mistake

with the fire, and the shelter they'd worked so hard to build?

There were no answers, of course. It was as if her brain had gone numb. All she could do now was sit on the cold sand in the dark, staring at their burned-out lean-to—and wonder how she was ever going to face the others again.

CHAPTER 14

It was just before dawn when the rain came.

There wasn't much of it—just a passing cloudburst. But the downpour was fast and hard enough to extinguish the small fire Buzz had managed to hold on to. A cloudy day seemed to be in the works. They still had the glass magnifier, but there would be no way to use it until the sun came out.

One step forward, two steps back, Buzz thought. Nothing was easy here. It felt like the island was working against them most of the time.

As the rain became a drizzle, and then a soft

mist, he stood up and stretched. He, Carter, and Jane had taken shelter under a tree, but Vanessa had stayed away. She'd kept to the beach all night.

Now, as Buzz looked down to the shore in the earliest morning light, he realized he couldn't see her anymore. The spot where she'd been sitting before was empty.

"Where's Vanessa?" he asked.

"I thought she was over there," Carter said, pointing.

"She was," Buzz said, "but she's not now."

"She can't be very far," Jane said. "We're not supposed to wander off. That's her rule."

"Maybe not for much longer," Carter said. He set a coconut on the ground by the fire pit and took a chop at it with the axe.

"What do you mean?" Buzz asked.

"I mean, maybe we need to think about a new leader," Carter said. With another swing, he took the top off the coconut and handed it to Jane to have the first drink. "That's all I'm saying."

But Buzz couldn't think about that right now. He

just wanted to find Vanessa and bring her back.

It was strange, how empty the camp seemed when one of them was missing. Especially Vanessa. At home, she had a million friends around her all the time. Even if she went to her room for a while, she'd be back downstairs hanging out with everyone else before long. Something about this didn't feel right.

Without a word to Carter or Jane, Buzz walked down to the water and then started up the beach to look for her.

He went slowly, keeping an eye out. Every minute or so, he turned all the way around, hoping to see Vanessa coming out of the woods, or hear her calling his name. But there was no sign of her anywhere.

The more Buzz thought about it, the more convinced he felt that something bad had happened. Maybe something very bad. They were going to have to get serious about looking for her, and soon.

Then, as he turned and started back, Buzz heard something. It was a foreign kind of sound. Nothing he recognized at first.

"Vanessa?" he shouted out again.

There was no answer, but the noise was still there. It was a humming of some kind in the distance. Or a buzzing. Or . . .

He turned and looked out toward the horizon. It took several seconds, but then he saw it. The small shape of a plane was crossing the sky—and coming straight toward the island.

Everything inside of Buzz seemed to speed up. He felt like his blood was suddenly running twice as fast as before. He jumped up and down, shouting and waving his arms.

"Hey! Hey! Over here!"

It was a useless impulse, he realized. Of course they couldn't hear him up there. They probably couldn't see him, either.

That's what the signal fire was for.

This was it. This was the chance they'd been hoping for. And that meant they had to get up to Lookout Point. *Now*.

With one more glance in the plane's direction, he took off at a sprint for camp.

Carter was just starting to tear down the burned-out shelter roof when Buzz came tearing up the beach.

"There's a plane!" he yelled. "A plane! A plane!"

By the time Carter realized what he'd said, Buzz had already run past him and up into the woods.

In the next moment, Carter was running, too. He sprinted into the jungle, leaving Jane behind. That didn't matter right now. Getting up there as fast as possible was all that counted.

He tore through the woods, past the cave, and then uphill again, pushing himself as hard as ever.

Buzz was struggling to climb up the gravel slope when Carter got there. The loose ground was sliding away under his feet, and he wasn't making much progress.

With several fast strides, Carter was up and past him, yelling to Buzz as he went.

"Where's the plane?" he asked without slowing down.

"Off the beach!" Buzz yelled back. "To the . . . east! East!" he said. "And I think it was coming this way!"

Everything inside of Carter funneled down into one, singular purpose: reach the signal fire and get it burning—ASAP.

He heard Jane now, too, running behind him. "Go, Carter!" she yelled. "Hurry!"

At the top of the slope, he cut right and ran toward the tree bridge as fast as the narrow ridge would allow. It was all familiar now. He had this. He could hear the soft humming of the plane in the distance. It was the sound of hope.

When he reached the tree, he yanked himself up through the exposed roots and out onto the trunk, heading across in a fast, low commando crawl. He could hear Jane and Buzz again, catching up behind him. They were on the tree bridge now, too, but he didn't even look back. His focus was straight ahead.

At the far end of the bridge, he scrambled down faster than ever and started to sprint through the last stretch of woods toward the open ground of Lookout Point.

But halfway there, a scream from Jane stopped him short.

When Carter turned to look, he saw that the ground holding up the nearest end of the tree bridge had begun to fall away. It was like a small avalanche of dirt and gravel. The tree itself had begun to slide right off the crumbling edge of the ravine.

Jane and Buzz were nearly all the way across, but still moving through the tree's branches. Jane was in front. She jumped the last several feet to land on solid ground just in time.

Behind her, Buzz wasn't so lucky. He jumped, too—and then disappeared over the edge, along with the tree itself.

For an instant, Carter's mind was divided. There was no way to get to the signal fire—their only chance of rescue—*and* to Jane and Buzz at the same time. But the thought had barely formed in his mind before he was racing back toward the ravine. Instinct made the choice for him. He had to save his brother if he could.

When Carter got there, Jane was already peering

over the edge. He threw himself on the ground next to her and looked down.

Buzz was there. He hung on the side of the ravine wall, maybe six feet below. Both of his hands were clasped around a lip of rock while he kicked at the wall, trying to find—or make—a toehold. His eyes were wild with fear.

"Hang on!" Carter yelled.

"I don't know if I can!" Buzz said.

In the background, the sound of the plane grew louder.

"Buzz, whatever you do—don't let go!" Jane shouted. She lay flat against the ground, reaching for him as far down the ravine wall as she dared. Still, it wasn't enough.

Carter couldn't reach him, either. "Can you climb?" he asked frantically.

Buzz reached for an exposed root over his head, but it was just beyond his grasp. When he collapsed back, dust and gravel showered down in his face before falling to the ravine floor a hundred feet below. At the bottom, Jane could see the tree that had been their bridge until now, lying there like a giant dead body.

"What should we do, Carter?" she asked. He was already up and looking around the immediate area. "Rope!" he said desperately.

"We don't have rope!" Jane said.

"Maybe this will work," he answered, tearing off his own shirt. "Hold on to me!"

Jane grabbed his legs as Carter threw himself down on the cliff's edge again and dangled the shirt.

"Buzz!" he yelled. "Can you reach this?"

Buzz strained for it, but his fingers barely whiffed at the cloth of the shirt. Above them, the sound of the plane was growing even louder. Carter scooted forward, inching his body a little farther over the edge.

"Carter, be careful! I can't hold you!" Jane yelled. If he went over, she'd never be able to stop him. They needed something longer. Something that Buzz could reach—and climb.

And then all at once, she realized what it was. "Use me!" she said.

"What?"

"Sit up!"

Carter scooted back up while Jane took his place. She backed herself over the lip of the ravine, feetfirst, and put her hands out for Carter to take.

"Lower me down there!" she said. "But don't let go!"

"That's crazy!" he said.

"Just do it," Jane said. "Lower me down! Right now!"

There wasn't any choice. Carter took both of her wrists and she grabbed onto his, and they locked themselves together.

"Buzz!" Jane yelled again. "Grab my feet."

"Jane, no!" he yelled. "It won't work!"

"Now!" she said.

"Yeah," Carter groaned out. "NOW!"

Carter had a good grip on Jane, but she could feel herself slipping lower than she wanted to be. He was going to have to pull them both back up.

At the same time, she could hear the plane—almost directly overhead now. But they were hidden in the ravine. A stand of scrubby trees shielded them from above. There was no way to be seen here. No way to catch the plane's attention without getting to that signal fire.

"I can't do this!" Buzz said.

"YES, YOU CAN!" Jane shouted. "Just do it— RIGHT NOW!"

She barely even recognized her own voice. It came from somewhere deep inside—never as strong as that before. Never so adult.

The next thing she felt was Buzz's hand on her ankle. Carter gripped her wrists at the other end— but his hold was slipping fast.

"PULL, CARTER—PULL!" she called.

There was a terrible tension in her body. Buzz held on to her legs from below while Carter dragged her in the opposite direction from above. She couldn't see Buzz, but she could feel him scrambling higher and searching for a foothold. For a moment, it felt as if she were about to snap in half. She squeezed her eyes shut, waiting for the worst. A sob caught in her throat.

And then, the tension eased. Buzz had found his foothold. He was climbing again, until he was at her side, pulling himself onto level ground.

At the same time, Carter yanked Jane up over the edge, and all three of them collapsed there, onto their backs.

Jane struggled just to catch her breath. "Too . . . close!" she said.

"No," Buzz panted out. He got up to his knees and pointed into the distance. The sound of the plane was still there, but growing fainter. "Not close enough," he said.

Carter forced himself onto his feet, and stumbled in the direction of Lookout Point. As long as they could still hear the plane, there was still some hope.

He staggered forward on wobbly legs, struggling to make a fast, straight line toward the open ground of the point. When he got there, the plane was still in sight, but no longer overhead. It had already started heading away from the island.

"HEY! HEY! DOWN HERE!"

Jane and Buzz were right behind now, screaming as well.

"HELP US!"

"STOP! COME BACK!"

Carter fell to his knees at the base of their six-foot-tall pile of twigs, branches, and palm fronds. He reached inside, pulled out the flare, and yanked off the cap. It began to spark and flame right away, igniting the smallest pieces of kindling.

He dropped the flare in the middle of the pyre and let the flames take over. The fire grew quickly, and started to grow taller. Hotter. Brighter.

"DOWN HERE! DOWN HERE!" Buzz and Jane continued to yell, jumping and waving. The plane was right there—still close enough for them to see its gray body and the dark blue markings on its wings and tail.

There were people inside that plane. People

who could help them. Water. Food. Rescue. *Turn around*, Carter thought. *Just turn around and look.*

But it was banking west now, heading back out over the ocean. For good.

"NO!"

"COME BACK!"

"STOP! PLEASE!"

It seemed impossible, but there was no denying it. *The plane was leaving.* It didn't matter how much shouting or waving they did anymore. A minute later, it was gone, almost as if it had never been there to begin with.

For a long time, nobody said anything or even moved. There were no words for the feelings Carter had. He knew he was going to cry. Eventually. But not right now. All he could really feel was the heat of the signal fire behind him. The whole thing had blazed up as quickly and intensely as they'd imagined it might.

Just not in time to save them.

Buzz felt numb. He stared at the empty sky where the plane had been just a minute ago, willing it to reappear. But of course, it didn't. Their one chance of rescue had just evaporated, like some kind of dream. Or a nightmare, really.

Finally, Jane stood up. Buzz stayed where he was. He followed her with his eyes as she walked to the edge of the point. She looked down for several seconds, then turned and walked slowly in the other direction, to gaze back through the trees toward the ravine.

"Jane?" Buzz asked. "What is it?"

She seemed to be thinking about something besides the plane. When she turned around again, there was a strange expression on her face.

"The tree bridge," she said.

"What about it?" Carter asked.

But Buzz realized right away what she meant. It came over him with a fresh wave of dread. The fact was, they already had a whole new problem to deal with. A big one.

There was a reason they'd built their signal

fire up here. Lookout Point was an isolated tower of rock, with views in every direction. There were no trails or paths leading up here—just steep cliffs and drop-offs on every side. Up to now, the only way to reach the point had been by crossing the tree bridge—the one that no longer existed.

And *that* meant they'd lost their only way down from this place.

CHAPTER 15

Vanessa stood on the rocks of an unfamiliar stretch of shore, staring at the last thing she'd expected to find here on Nowhere Island.

It was an old boat. It sat in a rocky clearing of the shore, at the foot of several tall lava cliffs. The boat must have crashed here, just like the *Lucky Star*—except this one had never left its resting spot.

It was hard to believe her eyes. She watched it from a distance for several minutes, just taking it all in.

She hadn't intended to be gone this long. Somewhere around sunrise, the unexplored shoreline had called to her. She'd climbed up onto Dead Man's Shelf, started picking her way across the rocks, and just kept going. It was a way to get off by herself for a little while—a chance to get her head together before she tried to face the others back at camp.

Now, here she stood, transfixed by what she'd found.

The boat was nearly twice as big as the *Lucky Star* had been. Vanessa didn't know much about this kind of thing, but it looked as if it had been built for carrying cargo of some kind. Not a pleasure craft, and definitely not a sailboat. But it was hard to tell any more than that.

It seemed to be made entirely of metal. The outside had turned halfway back to the colors of the earth around it, with a heavy coat of green algae on its rusted hull. If there had been a name painted on the side at some point, there wasn't anymore.

Then slowly, it dawned on Vanessa that the boat, however long it had been here, might still have something on board that they could use. Blankets, maybe. Tools. A tarp. Anything at all.

She had to work her way inland a little bit to get closer. She pushed through vines and fallen limbs, keeping an eye on the tiny bay to her right through the trees, looking for the best way to reach the boat.

As she came out of the woods again, it was onto a small spit of sand, not even big enough to be a beach. At the far end was a stream trickling down through a wide crack in the rocky shore. At the top of that were more woods on a level piece of ground overlooking the boat itself.

And if Vanessa wasn't mistaken, there was some kind of small structure up there. She squinted, trying to get a better look. It wasn't a building. It was a post of some kind—something in the ground. Definitely man-made.

"Hello?" she called out. The sound of her own voice in the silent cove startled her, and for a moment she forgot about the boat.

She worked her way up through the crevice in

the rocks, stopping long enough for a long, sweet drink of fresh water from the stream—her first in days. Then she climbed a little higher, until she was standing in a woodsy, sun-dappled clearing at the top.

There, sunk into the ground, was a crudely made wooden cross. It had no name or markings. It was just two planks with a single nail in the middle to hold them together. Vanessa's heart pounded as she took it in, considering what it all meant.

As her eyes traveled a few feet farther into the woods, she saw something else. Something much worse. Lying on the ground, under some number of years' worth of growth and decay, sat a skeleton. A *human* skeleton. Half covered as it was with leaves and fallen branches, there was still no mistaking the shape of it for anything else.

Vanessa staggered back. As she did, a fuller realization came to her. Whoever those people had been, they were trapped here on Nowhere Island, too.

And more than that, they'd never been rescued.

Without another look, she turned and ran back in the direction from which she'd just come. The new boat, the stream of fresh water—all of it would have to wait.

More than anything right now, she had to tell the others.

EPILOGUE

KONA, HAWAII—Progress on the search for the Benson-Diaz party from the missing *Lucky Star* has been slow, according to Coast Guard officials. Initial hopes were that the rescued captain and first mate of that vessel would be able to point rescue operations in the direction of the four missing children. So far, those efforts have proven unsuccessful.

Dexter Kingson and Joe Kahali, captain and first mate of the *Lucky Star,* say that they're thankful to be alive, but that their first concern has been, and remains, the Benson-Diaz family children— Vanessa Diaz, Benjamin "Buzz" Diaz, Carter

Benson, and Jane Benson.

Commander Carl Blakey of the U.S. Coast Guard expressed both relief at the recovery of Captain Kingson and Mr. Kahali, and also some continued hope that they will be able to offer unique assistance in the ongoing search.

"If anyone can figure out where the children might be, it's these guys," Blakey told reporters.

Search and rescue efforts continue daily.

READ THE ENTIRE SERIES!

STRANDED

STRANDED 2:
TRIAL BY FIRE

STRANDED 3:
SURVIVORS

THE STORY CONTINUES IN

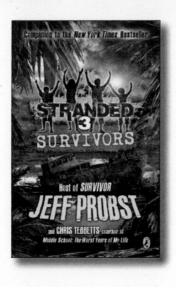

It's been days since Buzz, Vanessa, Carter, and Jane were stranded on a deserted island in the middle of the South Pacific. No adults. No supplies. Nothing but themselves and the jungle. And now they've lost their only shelter, and quite possibly their one chance at being rescued. Now the four kids must come together and delve even deeper into Nowhere Island for food and supplies if they're going to be able to survive. But the island has a few secrets of its own to tell. . . . With danger at every turn, this blended family has to learn how to trust one another if they stand any chance of survival.

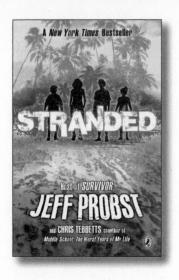

It was supposed to be a vacation—and a chance to get to know one another better. But when a massive storm sets in without warning, four kids are shipwrecked alone on a rocky jungle island in the middle of the South Pacific. No adults. No instructions. Nobody to rely on but themselves. Can they make it home alive?

A week ago, the biggest challenge Vanessa, Buzz, Carter, and Jane had was learning to live as a new blended family. Now the four siblings must find a way to work together if they're going to make it off the island. But first they've got to learn to survive one another.

JEFF PROBST (www.jeffprobst.com) is the multi-Emmy Award–winning host and executive producer of the popular series *Survivor*. He is also the founder of The Serpentine Project, a nonprofit organization designed to help young adults transition out of the foster care system, and has worked with the larger nonprofit organization Alliance for Children's Rights, which has provided one hundred thousand kids in Los Angeles with free legal assistance and advocacy. Each season, *Survivor* memorabilia is auctioned off, and, to date, the auctions have raised hundreds of thousands of dollars for the organization.

A native of Wichita, Kansas, Probst is married and lives in Los Angeles with his wife and two children when not traveling the world.

He can be followed on Twitter @jeffprobst and online at www.jeffprobst.com.

CHRIS TEBBETTS is the *New York Times* bestselling coauthor of James Patterson's Middle School series. Originally from Yellow Springs, Ohio, Tebbetts is a graduate of Northwestern University. He lives and writes in Vermont.